# Booth

# Booth

Timothy David Jones

# REQUIEM FOR A TINY SOLDIER

When Wesley Booth was 10 years old, he killed a mockingbird. Not a Harper Lee, Atticus Finch one, but a real baby mockingbird. It was just learning to fly and had no defense against the series of rocks launched from Wesley's slingshot. The weapon was crafted from a Y of crepe myrtle, two strips of inner tube and a canvas pouch. The first shot was a direct hit from 4 feet away that knocked the bird off its perch in the bush where it was trying out its wings.

It was the first bird Wesley had ever shot, and he was stunned—not only that he'd hit it, but that it didn't gracefully topple over dead. Instead, it fluttered wildly on the ground with its yellow beak opening and closing. His father had told him a good hunter never let an animal suffer, so, appalled at what he'd gotten himself into, he pulled back the rubber and let fly again. This rock hit the fledgling in the wing, spinning it around. It continued fluttering, but now with one wing dragging. Wesley fired again, and missed. The rock kicked dust into the bird's mouth. The seconds of reloading between shots were an eternal torment. Another shot, and Wesley could barely see with his flooded, blinking eyes. His mouth made desperate, hopeless little sounds as he ran to the driveway to scratch up more rocks with violent bleeding fingers.

When Wesley got back to the bush, the little bird had somehow struggled up and now stood on its twiggy legs, like a tiny condemned Confederate soldier. It was covered with dust. It just waited there, looking directly up into Wesley's streaming face as he reloaded the catapult. When he moved left for a better view, the bird shuffled around to face him with dislocated beak and uncomprehending black eyes.

Choking on the snot and damnation running down his throat, Wesley did what he had to do. This one got the little soldier hard, directly in the throat, and at last it lay done for, a fading shudder in the molecules of the Louisiana dust.

*...what follows is dedicated to that little soldier*

# *dignity*

*August 13, 1971. Alexandria, Louisiana*
*The State Employment Agency*

Wesley Booth stands fraudulently between a mismatched pair of crutches in this green tiled room, sweating amongst the unfortunate. Blue jeans too short and loafers with no socks. Tattered remains of an army fatigue shirt. The top of his long hair was pasted down with Brylcreem, the rest a humidity-frizzled poof around his ears and down over the collar. A pair of black-rimmed glasses sat on a nose both English and Cherokee. A piece of white surgical tape secured the broken right earpiece.

The line cleared gradually in front of him and he hopped slowly forward, a man on a stick. But with an accepting grimace on his face.

Just one more and then my turn. Fix my pained smile into place and prepare to lie pleasantly in case Mrs. Tanner asks

1

where I plan to look for work this week. It wouldn't do to tell the truth here. Imagine this little exchange:

*"Actually, I'll be looking up skirts."*

*"Pardon me?" Shocked, casting a Victorian look at my sweating face.*

*"Up skirts is where I'll be looking to work. Right there at the top, you know." Laughing lightly. "In the fur trade."*

But reality, and Mrs. Tanner was intent on business. She brought the tips of her fingers together, judicially.

"Mr. Booth. How good to see you again."

I hate it when they have the upper hand and look at me in that smirking way. "Mrs. Tanner. Good morning to you."

The woman stamped a voucher, then consulted a file. "Let's see...hmm, that's what I thought." She looked up, affecting a look of innocent puzzlement. "You received yo-wah final check last week, didn't you? Unless of course you've brought the documentation we need." She made the face of a schoolmarm prompting a slow student.

"Yo-wah medical records from the military. For verification of the service connected disability." Leaning heavily on the overworked charm of her antebellum accent, an irritating insistence upon adding a syllable to words ending with the letter *r*. And I smell an oppressive puff of floral powder.

Booth speaks again, in a most reasonable tone: "I'm afraid there's been a little snag...a tornado hit the records facility up in Omaha. Lightning touched off a fire..."

"Our records show that you haven't seen ow-ah medical evaluator yet, either."

"It's been very difficult for me to connect with the doctor. Some things have come up."

"Yes, I remember." Her nose pointing again at the sheaf of papers. "It says here you've broken six appointments with him."

"My mother's health, you know. The accident with the lawnmower..."

The woman abruptly put down her stamp, a sharp rap which made Booth jump. The other supplicants turning their heads to see. Mrs. Tanner then looked up with penetrating calmness into his eyes.

"Mr. Booth, I'm afraid the check you received last week was your final disbursement. That is, until we've been provided with proper confirmation of your condition, either by the military or by our medical evaluator. Now, if we receive confirmation, as I've told you before, then we can authorize the release of Title 7 emergency funds. But I think I can assure you that your application won't be approved unless you demonstrate a more cooperative attitude. In the meantime, I can only suggest that you find a job." A sardonic pause. "Something that won't tax yo-wah physical condition."

Her gray chin, summarizing the situation in this humiliating way. And light glinting dully from her teeth, dry and false. I feel the prickling of the others' eyes upon me, subjected to judgment here in the company of beggars. Best to leave with at least a shred of respect. This final communication, then, for the record.

Booth leaned down close. "Have you ever considered a cold coffee enema, Mrs. Tanner?" Her eyes popping wide behind the pearl glasses. "It can be done right in the home, and I've heard of some rather startling improvements in cases of speech impediment." A look of fear dawned across the woman's face. Booth turned with a degenerate dignity and swung on his crutches through the watching crowd.

Out this fatal door then. Nothing in the hand but air, and a white haze of Louisiana heat bearing insufferably down. With a rash of sweat breaking across his forehead, Booth lit up a Winston and blew on the tip. Crumpled the empty red and white package and tossed it into an alley.

These awful impediments to my destiny. People pawing at me at every turn; forms to fill out and assurances to be mulled. Intense scrutiny focused on my every declaration and now the nightmare prospect of actually having to take a job. And my mother with one waiting for me, too. Some church friend named Malone offering something. Something menial, no doubt, and menial is a word I find most distasteful. But they only give you six months worth of unemployment. A small price to pay, I should think, for keeping me away from people who work for a living. I seem to annoy those who work, and they annoy me. I think I'd be better off out west. Albuquerque, maybe, or Flagstaff.

He crutched up the street on his unemployment props, bought for a dollar at the Salvation Army. Around the corner, out of sight, he pitched them into the back seat of his mother's '62 Biscayne, loaned to him in a motherly faith that he was out looking for doors of opportunity.

Booth started the car and turned the air conditioner on full. He glanced in the side mirror as he pulled away from the curb.

"God *damn* it." Booth's hand scrabbled under the seat for a can of warm beer, eyes staring into the mirror.

Above the oak trees, towards the southwest, the knuckled white fist of a Louisiana thunderhead poked teasingly into the cellophane blue of the sky.

—ɯ—

A short while later, Booth types a light stanza:

*That fatal quill*
*touches down again*
*And spills a life*
*in bloody*
*scratches*

"Wesley?" A call from the hallway, accompanied by tapping. A perfectly calculated intrusion.

Booth's brow furrows in irritation, fingers poised over the dished black keys. "Yeah, Mom."

"I wonder if you could run a couple of errands for me."

"Errands?" I don't know what it is about that little word that makes me feel so much like murder. The simple distraction from my work is bad enough, but that particular word, fat with servility and insinuation, actually makes my scrotum shrivel. And outside this window I can see the world dying lushly of heat and suffocating humidity.

"Uh, what exactly would those be, Mom?" His bare shoulders hunched and gray eyes sliding sideways, halfway to the door. The jaw slung slightly open, the way one does. "I *am* trying to write in here." He touches the Remington Rand, taps out a word. *Frangible.*

"Well, I was hoping maybe you could drop by Fran's and pick up those dress patterns for me."

Booth picks up a distressed Silvertone guitar, punched the power button on a failing Haynes amplifier and ripped off a biting blues lick in B pentatonic minor, loudly. "Is that it, then?"

"Well, while you're out there do you think you could bring

McGee back with you?" Her voice higher, and with a certain tone.

It's never just the one thing. Always something else tacked onto the original request, another item to be ticked off. "Mom, you know what happens every time I get around that damned bird. I sneeze for hours. And last time the thing went right for my eyes. It's just plain vicious."

"Oh, she is not. She was just curious about the beads on that headband of yours." A pause. "Wesley, I really do wish you wouldn't use that kind of language in this house."

"Oh, no more English?"

"You know what I mean..."

"Frankly, Mom, I never heard of anybody sharing a parakeet before. It's a little odd, if you ask me. I mean I could see it if it was a dog, maybe, or some kind of ape, but birds are small and cheap. Everybody can have one of their own."

"You don't need to be ugly, Wesley. We take turns teaching her words, that's all. If you don't want to go, just say so."

"I don't want to go."

"Well *fine*, then. If you can't do a simple little errand..."

He switched off the power on the amplifier. Laid down the guitar. "All right, all right. I was just kidding, Mom." He opened the door and put his hands on her shoulders, small and fragile and, probably, easy to disjoint. *Frangible.* Just like preparing a chicken for dinner. He placed his thumbs experimentally on the knobs. See her moist eyes, wide with a rabbit kind of fear.

"You always take it so seriously when I poke a little fun."

"Well, you're so strange lately. Your door's always shut and all you do is play that guitar."

"Or write. I write, Mom..."

"You hardly ever even talk to me anymore." She pulled away with a grimace. "And it smells like you've been drinking again."

"Drinking?" A shocked expression. "That's what you say every time you see me. You know how hard it is for me to concentrate since the war. I need focus. For my work."

"The war was in Vietnam, Wesley. You were at Fort Meade the whole time."

"But that's exactly my point. While all the troops were over there fighting, who was up in Baltimore keeping the hippies in line?"

"The hippies...?"

"Protesters, Mom, demonstrators. The underclass went stone crazy up there. I was nearly killed twice."

"What do you mean, *you* were nearly killed? I never heard you say anything about that."

"It was while I was on riot duty...too nasty to talk about, really..." He turned away, eyes squinched, hand up for a sneeze.

*"Achooey!!"* Looking at the hand. "Good grief. Look at this, Mom."

"*Oh don't you dare! Wesley!*" Fleeing down the hallway, her heels clipping on the hardwood floor.

"Just kidding, Mom. God, you're jumpy." He stepped into the bathroom, reeled off a wad of toilet paper to blow his nose. "How about a little money for gas?"

"The tank should be full. I just filled it up yesterday."

"Oh, okay, no sweat."

On his way through the kitchen Booth spies his mother's purse, luckily left on the drain board. Deftly steals a loose five dollar bill, faking a coughing spasm to cover up the snapping of the clasp. "See? Just thinking about that bird has got me started."

His mother sits down on the sofa, smoothing out a doily. "Have you given any thought to that job interview with Mr. Malone tomorrow?"

A flash of dread, hooded and fanged. But...

"To tell you the truth I'm anxious to get started. I think I can go a long way in that position." He turned to face her with widened eyes and a reverent inflection. "Why, I understand they even have profit sharing."

She looked at him narrowly. "Don't be a cynic, Wesley. How long do you think you can go without a job? You've been home what, seven months now and you know I can't keep up with things here without some help."

Booth bent over at the picture window and looked up through the pine trees. The top of a thunderhead, looming starkly against an otherwise unsullied sky. He sucked in a breath and blew it out.

"Listen...you know I'm only taking this to get me by until I hook up with a band. Or get one of my stories published. One other thing. We need to talk about that car loan since I'm getting a job. I called Mr. Prine down at the bank and he said it was no problem as long as you co-sign the note."

Her features took on a look of distaste. "I can't believe you're even *thinking* about playing in a band, Wesley. You never made any money doing that before the army. And that racket you all made was just the worst stuff I ever heard."

He pinched her cheek gently between his thumb and a knuckle. "Rock and roll is here to stay, Mom, whether you like it or not."

She pulled away and cleared her throat. "There's a letter for you. On the piano."

A manila envelope, with a crease of having been folded. And

I recognize the handwriting, and those stamps. The return address stamped there. HMH Publishing. Chicago.

"What is it? It felt heavy." His mother feigning benevolent ignorance.

With his back to his mother, Booth's nervous fingers ripped at the envelope, seeking deliverance. He had submitted a recent story about a man and a bear, the publication of which might show his mother and the others his substance and destiny. Bring about an end to this pestering.

Out slide his several pages of typing, along with a blue slip of paper. A particularly cheap grade of type on the note.

He read silently:

We regret that we are unable to use your submission in our publication at the present time for the reason checked below. Thank you for your interest in Playboy and good luck in your future endeavors

Tone wrong for our magazine

Subject matter too similar to others already included

Style incompatible with our format

No reason was checked. The back of the slip was blank.

"Well, what is it?"

This small hand clutching at my throat.

"Oh, just a response from an editor." He walked out of the room. "I'll be right back."

In his room, he shoved the envelope into a desk drawer with the others. Tore the rejection slip into small pieces and put them into the pocket of his jeans. Back into the living room.

"Well, are they going to print the story?"

"As a matter of fact, they're thinking about working it into an anthology..."

"With that one you told me about last month?"

"Ah...yes, but there's a little editorial stuff that we have to do on that one..."

"Here's another letter. It looks sort of official." This one brown, with a cellophane window, and his name there. Opening this one slowly.

*U.S. Government*
*Department of the Army*
*Office of Personnel Records*

*Dear Mr. Booth:*

*Regarding correspondence from the Louisiana State Employment Agency.*

*A request was made recently by the above agency for medical records corroborating your claim of a service connected disability. A search of our records shows no such material on file. Above agency has been notified of this finding by letter dated 10 August.*

*Government policy requires this office to include the following statement:*

*It is a violation of Federal law to make untrue statements in order to obtain funding which proceeds in all or in part from Federal monies. This includes making false statements to the effect that any condition or state exists which would, if true, entitle one to said monies.*

*Sincerely,*
*Marlin Twill, Ass't. Director*

Monies. Money. Lucre. Filthy, and elusive, as well. Now the Feds on my trail, along with the others. But I don't think they can prove I actually meant to defraud. There truly is a condition, after all. Possibly a point of confusion at the employment agency...

*"Wesley, are you listening to me?"*

Blinking. "What?" He stuffed the letter back in the envelope.

"I said, could you try and be back here by five? Remember we're going to Evelyn Bachmeier's for dinner tonight and I've got to go shopping for salad stuff." The sound of planning and assumption here, and also that of being ignored.

"What's this *we* business? I don't think *I've* got any plans like that. *I'm* planning on writing tonight."

"Don't tell me you don't remember. You said last Saturday you'd go. Evelyn's got her niece visiting, and I thought it'd be nice..."

"Last Saturday? Ok, I remember it clearly now. You've got it all mixed up. What I said was that I'd rather go almost anyplace than there." He paused. "This smells like another one of your tries at setting me up, Mom. I've told you I don't like that. Remember the Earlene incident?"

"No it's not. And Earlene is a perfectly nice girl, Wesley..."

"She's like my first cousin, Mom. You don't find that a little odd? A little...incestuous?"

"She's a third cousin, twice removed. And besides, you'd never met her..."

"She wasn't so bad, really. But I was put off by a few things. Don't you remember what I told you? How she embarrassed me?"

"Embarrassed you?"

"Frankly, Mom, she's flatulent..."

*"Oh, Wesley, for gosh sakes.* That's just plain ugly..."

"...and it's not just the noises I'm talking about, either."

"Oh just stop it. My God..."

Booth forms a chord on the piano, plays a discordant riff. "So what's the big deal about me going over there?"

"No big deal at all, just that you haven't seen Evelyn since you've been home, and she always asks about you."

"Look, Mom, I better get out of here if I'm going to get back in time."

"Then you'll go?"

"Sure, as long as you're paying me."

"I'm not going to pay you, Wesley. Why are you acting like this?"

"I'm just kidding, Mom. But I would appreciate it if you'd loan me twenty bucks. I need some new clothes for that interview." He reaches for his crutches.

"You mean give you twenty. You still owe me that ten dollars from last week...and why are you still using those crutches, anyway? I've seen you outside..."

"The army doctors told me to exercise lightly, but not to excess..."

"Tell me again what you say is wrong with you?"

"Retained umbilicus. Wrapped around my spine."

"That's ridiculous and you know it. I really hope you don't show your ignorance by telling that to anybody else..."

"Mom, getting back to this little loan...how can I pay you back without a job? And how can I get a job if I show up at the interview looking like some kind of wastrel? It's only twenty dollars we're talking about here, not the national budget."

She paused, then blinked. "Bring me my purse, then. I really do need this back, Wesley."

In the kitchen, he stuffed the five back in quickly, evading discovery. A smell of lipstick and Kleenex and Green Stamps. He hands her the purse.

"Oh...just one more thing while you're out..." Her head bent down, hand stirring in the bag.

"Yeah? Now what?" Booth stands still, a feel of coiling within.

"I'll sign that car note Monday, Wesley..." She straightened up with solemn eyes and held a twenty dollar bill out in the air between them.

"But today I want you to go by and see Howard." She took off her glasses and looked up at him, her chin set resolutely.

"It's just not right, and you know it."

Booth drives tensely through the floral casserole of a central Louisiana afternoon, half a six-pack of Schlitz on the floor of his mother's Biscayne, a stream of Winston smoke flowing out the wind-wing. And McGee the jointly-owned parakeet in the back seat. Melancholy words of Grand Funk Railroad on the radio, with the desolate cries of seagulls interspersed:

*...I'm getting closer to my home...*

McGee making a chirp. Beats me how the hell they know it's a female. Never laid an egg and I feel sure no one's picked through those feathers looking for a little bird pecker. Details like that come up. *Bird pecker.* Could easily be confused with the beak, I think, in idle conversation, and that is the kind in which I'm usually involved. Rather an absurd name for a bird, anyway.

A radio announcement now about the weather, delivered in a jovial disk jockey voice:

"*Hey, hey, looks like we're in for a little weather this PM. About a ninety percent chance of the wet stuff, along with the possibility of a few heavy thunder boomers. Woo, I don't know about you, but that's enough to make me batten down the hatches. Maybe curl up with a good book and a side of the slow stuff on the...*" A violent twist of the knob to shut him up, glancing nervously at the sky.

This pestilent, steaming place. Air the consistency of warm chicken fat. Pardon me while I step outside for a broth of fresh air.

My fragile life, or at least my sanity, staked on the caprice of these uncounted wafting molecules, poised as they are to roil into thunderstorms at the very hint of the right condition, menacing with black omen and threat of wildness. Me huddled under pillows at night to block out the flashes and muffle the windscream and banish the horrid phantasm of a pendant tornado, writhing from the clouds like a live snake in the taunting hand of a bully.

The thing that I find most irritating is that the others pay no attention at all to such a warning, lost in their little worlds of oblivion and bliss. Hear them say things like "Oh, I just love a good spring storm, don't you? The air's so nice and clear afterwards." Or just the disinterest itself, a burr under my saddle. Makes me want to take them by the windpipe. Smile bravely, though, and soldier on, as we usually do. Hope for the best, keep the fingers crossed tightly.

But now the sound of McGee acting up in the back seat. Plucking the wires of its cage musically and making noises as though trying to speak.

A quaver to Booth's voice as he attempted fellowship. "Say flatulent, McGee. Flat-u-lent. Come on, you little fucker. How about fraudulent, then."

Reach back over the seat with trembling finger to tap the cage in friendly encouragement.

"Say feculent, McGee, fec...*Ouch!*" The car swerved sharply. *"God damn it!* The thing had bitten him. Finger in his mouth, then spitting, fear of bird mites in the bloodstream. He picked up one of the dress patterns and lashed McGee's cage with it, producing a burst of tissue streamers, wild fluttering in the cage.

Throw the damned thing out the window, then. Treat a fellow creature with a little kindness and see what happens? Crank this Chevy up to about a hundred and ten and then *poof*, a green and yellow cloud of McGee feathers receding in the rearview mirror. Tell my mother that the air conditioner quit and when I rolled down the window to avoid suffocation the bird unfortunately got sucked into the slipstream. Cleverly replace a good fuse with a bad one to lend credibility to my sniffling tale.

With my current luck, though, the miraculous little bastard would show up anyhow, in a half-denuded state, with wounded eyes and long beak hanging in an accusing manner, having suddenly found full voice due to high speed asphalt trauma...

And now this. This benign, unholy place.

Booth turned into a broad and picturesque estate, gloom hanging greenly over pleasant pathways and spiked iron fence. A wide black man here at the gate, holding out a clipboard for me to sign. See his cigar and his sweat and the revolver on his belt, tiny and unnecessary. Booth scribbles his name and address on the form.

The purpose of my visit? Just dropping by for a chat with the dead, sir. My mother insists that I do this every now and then just to keep me from bursting into my little song of joy.

"Could you tell me where Ward D is?" A breathless quality to the voice. "I have an appointment to visit someone."

The man pointed. "Take this first left here, Cap'n. You'll see it on your right."

This brick building, then, fresh white trim but the mortar green with mold creeping up from the fungal soil. A sign above the door saying Ward D. Park here in the shade of this oak to preserve the parakeet's little life. Leave the radio on to keep it company as his mother insisted. But tune it to a twangy country station to annoy it.

Booth gets out and stretches nervously. He could hear the sound of a lawnmower rotating distantly around some corner. The leading shadow of the thunderhead moved over, raising a susurrus of insects and separating the colors of the flowers. Azaleas, I believe they are called. Booth looked up with fore-boding, taking a breath of the dead air. Get inside quickly.

At the desk a nurse, watching my eyes in a nervous way, and again my name required. Also, with a touch of suspicion, my relationship. In fact, demanding the driver's license to prove it. Typing identification on a badge form while Booth hangs between his crutches.

"I'm sorry, Mr. Booth. I hope you understand."

Pin the badge on carefully with its plastic holder. Now crutching down the darkly paneled hallway to room number 5. The nurse knocks on the door.

Why can't they ever get rid of this smell of piss in the hall-ways at least? That's something I've never fully understood. It would seem a simple thing to have the air analyzed by a competent professional, synthesize the appropriate antidote, and pump a heavy mist of the stuff through the ductwork. The nurse knocks again.

In view of this agonizing delay I think that perhaps there's no one home here. Went to shit and the hogs ate him, as they say. Just turning to mention this possibility to the nurse but she turns a key in the lock and opens the door just the same.

And now Booth raises his face fearfully to meet the eyes of his twin brother, Howard. And see his sallow stubbled face. Standing near the dresser in a hospital gown, with brows slightly raised as if surprised. A speckle of drool can be seen at the corner of his mouth. The nurse wipes it away with a kind word, using a wash cloth.

Booth moves into the room with a quaver of good will.

"Hey, Howard. Good to see you, man." Sit down here on this beige vinyl chair from the fifties, careful not to rip the pants on an upturned edge of petrified plastic, a tuft of stuffing poking out.

Howard paces rapidly, cheeks blowing out with air, look of anxiety on his face. Booth looks at the nurse with puzzled brow.

Nurse, patiently. "That's his place where you're sitting. He usually sits there."

Booth moves to the bunk to sit again. "This one OK? I mean, I'm not sure of the rules here."

"There's only one rule, really, Mr. Booth. Just talk quietly and please don't upset him. Ring this buzzer when you want to leave." And leaving us here in silence.

Booth makes his eyes look at his brother. "Well, how's everything going, man?" A doomed attempt at light conversation.

Booth looks around to see if anything's changed since last time, and sees that it has not. A sidelong glance at Howard's short haircut and Librium eyes, looking in a distracted way at my larynx. Never tried to hurt anyone at all, as well as I can remember.

Try a bit of reading as a device to establish rapport:

"Look here, Howard," thumbing through a Life magazine, "They've got a thing in here about the Beatles. About all the women they're supposed to have screwed, although they don't come right out and say it like that. Now that's what I call a revelation, don't you? The notion that rich rock and roll stars might hump out of wedlock?"

And so on about the war, the other newsworthy events of the world for twenty minutes, Howard just staring in the fashion of the classically deranged, softly humming that same unnamed tune he's been humming for the last 2 years. Something like *Old Dan Tucker*, but with a demented, Arabian lilt.

There was a deep boom of thunder, making Booth's nerves jerk. Howard's expression remained fixed, but the humming grew louder.

"Oh, hey. Have I told you I'm thinking of heading out west? Flagstaff, to be exact. You remember when we passed through there back in '67, on that trip with Mom? Well, it kind of stuck on me, and I thought I'd check it out. A lot cooler out there, which makes sense. Seven thousand feet up. None of this sticky, balmy feel there. Makes it worthwhile to dry off after your morning shower."

Booth notices his knee jumping. Take this opportunity to get out of here with my eyes and veins still intact. Standing up, stretching nonchalantly, pressing the button for the nurse.

"Well, Howard, I've gotta go, OK? Tell you what. After I check the place out I'll come get you and we can set up shop out there, huh? I understand there's a severe shortage of eligible bachelors."

Go over shyly to put an arm around Howard's unyielding shoulders for a measured moment as one is obliged to do under these circumstances. Feel a warm tear wetly on my cheek. Stand again to wait for the nurse, facing the door, swallowing and breath blowing through lips tightly, eyes awash and blinking.

Suddenly Howard's sour breath on my cheek and the pressing of his groin against my leg, an erection pulsing through his gown. Push him away, shocked and ashamed, sweet Jesus please save me. And my back against the dresser.

Howard comes back, a look of spastic, canine intent on his face and the tongue moving behind open, flaked lips. *"Unh unh, Howard. Come on, man."* An elbow raised to ward him off, and press this God damned button again and again. Booth shrieked. *"Shit!"* Yanking on the door knob.

Now the door swings open, bumping Booth's cheekbone, and the nurse comes in, saying, "OK, Howard, OK, now." Guiding him back to his place on the beige chair, a distressed sound from his upturned and drooling mouth, then a loud, sudden yelp like when a garrote is jerked tight.

Out the door and down the hall blindly. Away from this ordinary, demonic place, anguished heels scuffling on the cold checkered tiles. His crutches swung hard and banged against a potted begonia, the eruption of loam punctuating his fraud and his flight.

Booth flees out the front door into freakish wind and crack of thunder, the oak and pines waving stiffly under a malignant sky. A torrent roaring on the asphalt as he dashed to the car in a humping run, shirt and hair drenched and clinging. Into the car booming with noise, his breath leaking out in a whine, arms wrapped sobbing around the steering wheel and snot falling down.

Sharp, intensifying rain whipped the car and wind squealed at the windows. Booth wedged himself cowering under the dashboard, fingers in his ears and his mouth screaming softly to stop and stop. The radio turned up, pleasant infuriating chatter and bursts of lightning-static, the idiot chortling of McGee.

Bloody water of my sane and peaceful eyes. Keep them squeezed shut and straight ahead or else see those winged things, flapping and gargling joyfully around Howard in that dark nest in there. The leather headband fell to the floor with Indian beads, Booth's lip twisted wetly on his wrist.

In ten minutes, the squall tapered off, and Booth uncoiled himself and looked around in trembling shame, terrified eyes scanning the clouds for funnel shapes. He pulled himself up behind the wheel and placed his hands at the 10 o'clock and 2 o'clock positions.

When I die, and they drag me in front of that kangaroo court called Judgment Day, God or one of the others will ask me some leading questions concerning my behavior and how well I abided by the rules. After they've toyed with me a bit for the sheer sport of it, they'll take a moment to regain their dignity and dry their eyes, and then they'll get down to the nub of things. God himself will point His finger, shaking with rage, and ask me the question planned long in advance to punch my ticket into writhing Hell. This is what He will say:

*"Wesley Booth, did you keep your brother well?"*

—ɯ—

*Pass Christian Miss., August 20, 1969 (UPI)*

*A young man was found alive in the cab of a derrick crane here in the wake of Hurricane Camille. Rescuers here call it a miracle.*

*Pineville, Louisiana resident Howard Booth, 22, is recuperating in St. Regis Hospital after being found battered and suffering from exposure in the cab of a derrick crane just east of Pass Christian. His condition is guarded, but he's expected to make a full recovery, according to a hospital spokesman.*

*Booth and some friends were attending a hurricane party at a beach house in Pass Christian, but the car was apparently caught by the storm surge when the hurricane became too intense and they tried to drive to safety. The car was located a quarter-mile from the crane, but its owner, Richard Pearson, and the other two occupants, Roland Wiley and Shirley Descant, all from Alexandria, Louisiana, are still missing and presumed drowned.*

*Booth had apparently tied himself in the cab to keep from being blown out by Camille's rampaging 170 mph winds.*

# *september 22, 1957*

San Leon, Texas. Land's end. And a predatory wind booming in your face, pushing you around like after school with all the teachers gone home.

Overhead, there was the brief piping of a small bird in the chaos of its blown-away flight. Thin and plaintive and gone.

The hundred yards of reeds and sedge in the estuary separating the houses writhed green and brown, cyclic waves rolling in the fresh gale blowing in from the northeast. Facing the water, the houses themselves squatted rectangular and utilitarian, with similarly screened porches and rolled bamboo awnings, precautionary squares of scrap plywood nailed like Band-Aids over the windows. This house was yellow, the other, owned by neighbors named Higgins, was cadaver blue.

Under a baleful and descending sky, the water of Galveston Bay had taken on the color of slate, stark with menace. Beyond the small bluff that dropped off to the muddy sand of the beach, the gaunt pilings of Higgins' pier, currently under re-construction, stretched away to a desolate prospect, dots and hyphens far out in the throat of the squall. Farther still, a shrimp boat with rakish cabin wallowed low in the surge, working northward by desperate inches. The smoke of its exhaust streamed away to the south in a clotted, horizontal ribbon of grey. Within seconds, the boat was consumed by the bleak phalanx of rain that was eating inexorably, and rapidly, toward the beach.

A rippling crack of thunder as ten year old Wesley Booth bailed out the passenger door of the blue and white 1955 Ford Fairlane, leaped a wind riffed puddle and raced for the house, sneakers scarfing on the white shell driveway. He and Howard hit the door just as the leading pellets of rain caught up. They burst, tussling, into the kitchen with Uncle Jim right on their tail, head down, clutching paper bags full of supplies. Slamming the door and rain raking the house in a furious deluge.

"Woo-hoo! It's a comin' *down*, boys. Rainin' tadpoles." Uncle Jim took a Chesterfield out of his mouth and Wesley could see the brown spot where a single raindrop had landed on the cigarette. Lightning flashed again, catching Uncle Jim's features in theatric profile as he looked out into the torrent.

Aunt Lila and Howard sat at the kitchen table, elbows on yellow formica, setting up the board for checkers. Wesley hoisted a can of kerosene onto the table with a clunk.

"Hey, Aunt Lila, look at this." Howard dug into one of the bags of hurricane supplies: Hershey's cocoa mix, a pair of batteries, marshmallows, crackers, cheese and a new Monopoly set, the makings of haven and warmth. A red candle with a price sticker rolled into the depression where a 6 inch flake of the formica had delaminated years ago from the plywood. He pulled out several sheets of paper.

"Hurricane maps."

Uncle Jim put his bags down. "Better do some nursing here, baby. I had to send this soldier up underneath the car. Starter got hung up again."

"Come here, honey." She took Howard by the arm and turned him toward her. "Let's see your arm." A small patch of red showed above the wrist, a smudge of chalky white on his shoulder. "Shame on Uncle Jim, making you go under that hot car like that. And on those shells, too." She dusted off his shirt and examined him, aiming an inflection of indictment at Uncle Jim for the sake of bonhomie.

"It doesn't hurt anymore. Anyways, all I had to do was bang the starter." A casual look of boyish pride.

"Well, let's get another shirt on you, anyway. You've got a little rip here." Her pink finger with its short red fingernail poking through to show. She examined the arm again. "I'm going to put a little Vaseline on there just the same."

Uncle Jim turned away from the grey window of rain and his lips made a tiny pop as he spit out a speck of loose tobacco. "Sorry about that exhaust pipe, buddy. I need to keep you boys here all the time. That way you can take turns smacking the thing for me. It's too hard to reach from the top." He winked at Howard.

"Or else you could just get it fixed." Aunt Lila's gentle look of admonition.

"No point in fixing what's not broke. And I figure it's not broke if you can bang on it and make it go. Besides, it only happens every coupla weeks." He tweaked Aunt Lila's cheek playfully. "Say, baby, how about a beer?"

Outside the house the storm lunged, then retreated, a reiterate and mounting symphony of siege.

"Hey. Come look at this. There's a light out there." Howard calling from the window.

Wesley dragged his chair up next to his brother and looked through a shredded knothole in the plywood. Out there, it was all bluster and gloom, almost dark. The water of the bay thrashed wild and dangerous, waves heaving, plumes of spray bursting up from the concrete mooring of Higgins' pier.

Howard pointed. "See?"

About fifty yards out on the pier swung a solitary light, dancing like a lynched angel.

They all took turns silently looking until Aunt Lila said, "How in the world...?"

"Jim, why don't you give them a call? It's probably a good idea to keep in touch, with the weather like this."

"To hell with 'em. Coupla rich ninnies, anyway." He took a long pull at his bottle of Falstaff. "Don't worry, that light ain't gonna last long. Anybody want to bet on how long it stays there?"

The bets ranged from a few minutes to an hour. Howard was the only one to favor the light. He bet it would stay there all night.

Aunt Lila picked up the phone, untwisting the frayed fabric of the cord. "Well I'm going to call them anyway. You're such a poop about them..."

Wesley stood on the chair, looking out into the gray wrath of the storm. He could hear the clicking as his aunt dialed a number.

There was a long pause, then Aunt Lila said, "There's nothing on the phone."

"Was there a dial tone?" Uncle Jim was lighting another cigarette.

"I didn't notice." She pressed the button with her finger and released it.

"Nothing. There's no sound at all."

"Well it's out then." He took the receiver and tapped at the button. "Yep, dead as a door nail. I guess we're on our own."

Wesley looked again at the light out there on the pier. It waved wildly in the wind, lighting up the waves that wallowed and writhed like demons in a pit. He could see that they were rolling over the deck of the pier.

The light was the bravest and loneliest thing he'd ever seen.

Just then, the electricity went out. The sound of the wind got wilder in the silence left by the death of the refrigerator. Something pinged off the gutter outside.

There were commands and questions in the dark until Aunt Lila finally got a candle lit. Several more, then the kerosene lamp. The place felt like a Catholic church Wesley had been in once. Howard discovered a puddle of water the size of a basketball backboard by the front door.

But the light on Higgins' pier remained on. Uncle Jim grunted and said the only explanation was that the Higginses had finally got that generator they'd been talking about.

An hour and fourteen minutes later, the leather-cased transistor radio announced this:

*As of 6 PM, the eye of Hurricane Denise was located at 29 degrees North, 91 degrees West, about 200 miles south-southeast of Galveston. Denise now appears to be heading north-northwest at about 15 miles an hour. In addition to high winds, torrential rains and high tides should be expected as Denise approaches the coast. The Coast Guard*

*has issued a small craft advisory for the coast of Texas
from Corpus Christi to the mouth of the Sabine River...*

Aunt Lila looked at Uncle Jim, her brows drawn together.

"Hmm. That doesn't sound too good, does it, Jim? What do
you think? You know Catherine and Roger told us to come up if
we needed to."

"Ah, hell, you know how they are. Slightest little change and
they make a big deal out of it." He stood up and stretched
casually. "Still, we could maybe give it some thought..."

Ten minutes later, the sound of the Ford's engine, civil and
throbbing, a cradle of protection against the feral intent of the storm.
And the beery look on Uncle Jim's face as he turned around and
wiped his forehead in the glow of the dome light. He grinned. "This
is a little silly, boys. Gettin' all het up over a little weather. Like as not
it'll peter out now and we coulda stayed right here." A touch of relief,
however, if not outright glee, in his demeanor of escape.

Aunt Lila voicing an opinion. "Well, I'm just as glad to be
going. We would have been fine, but you never really know how
bad these things can get." An apostrophe of wet hair curved
darkly under her jaw. "Hadn't we better get going? We've got
about half an hour to League City."

"Just letting it warm up a minute, baby. Hate to run an engine cold."

A monolithic bolt of lightning stood suddenly and persis-
tently out over the water, a triumphant blue spike, apparently
connected to one of the near pilings of Higgins' pier. Its thunder
was a concussive, ripping blast. A sudden intake of breath by
Aunt Lila. Uncle Jim pulled the gearshift summarily up into
reverse and let out the clutch, killing the engine.

He sat for a moment as if stunned, then reached for the key and twisted it. Nothing. Turned off the headlights and twisted the key again. Nothing. "God damn it." His shoulders slumped in disbelief as he repeated the ritual. Not even a click.

Finally he said over his shoulder, "Hand me that tire iron, Wesley."

"The tire iron...?" Wesley squirming to feel.

"On the floorboard, damn it, right under your feet."

"You don't need to go off at the kids, Jim."

Wesley located the tool under the seat and handed it over.

Uncle Jim took a breath. The sound of the wind sawed with a mocking whine through the silence in the car. "Let me see that flashlight, Lila. Slide over here and try to crank it when you hear me hit the starter."

Uncle Jim struggled back into his yellow slicker and opened the door. Rain splattered the dash in the dimness of the dome light as Aunt Lila squirmed across the seat.

Lightning flashed and Wesley could see Howard curled up against the opposite door, his jacket up over his head, co-cooned. A wrenching sound and the hood rose up, Uncle Jim's slicker flapping in the void. Now the sound of the tire iron pecking feebly at a casting. Aunt Lila twisted the key, again and again, to no avail. She turned the rearview mirror so she could see into the back seat. "Are you all right, Howard?"

"When are we going to go?" His muffled voice faintly.

"As soon as your uncle gets the car started." She twisted the mirror around so Wesley could see her eyes. "I swan. I've asked him about this thing three times..." A fiendish gust of wind rocked the car. Howard made another whimper.

Presently Uncle Jim's face appeared from behind the hood,

distorted by the rain flooding over the windshield, his hair plastered to his scalp. Lightning flared and he could be seen, but not heard, shouting a command, gesturing with one hand while the other worked at something in the engine compartment. Aunt Lila twisted the key again and the dome light dimmed. Suddenly there was a yellow flash under the hood, then another. Uncle Jim jerked his arm up, his face illuminated in alarm, and Wesley heard metal clang into the underside of the hood. Uncle Jim jumped away, shaking his left hand in pain as a shower of sparks streaked away in the wind. He made a frantic lunge into the guts of the car, then desperately back to the door. A blast of wind and Uncle Jim's rage filled the car as he plowed in, grabbing for the key and shoving Aunt Lila across the seat.

*"Goddamn son of a bitch fucking thing. I swear to Christ! Why didn't you turn the fucking ignition off?"* Wesley's eyes wide, a painful knot in his throat, Howard's smothered whine in the corner.

"My God, Jim. The boys…" Her back was up against the door.

"Goddamn it. Well, we're screwed for sure now." He paused, breathing in sobs of air, his lips sucking on the back of his left hand. "Why didn't you turn off the key? Couldn't you see the sparks?" He sounded like he might cry.

"It's just not fair to blame me, Jim. I've asked you three times to get that thing fixed…"

"I can tell you for sure you don't want to get started with that." Another flash of lighting over the bay, a cold floret of gray embedded in the clouds. "Come on, boys. Let's get back inside. I guess we're gonna find out first hand how bad this damned thing is."

"Are you sure it won't start?"

"There's not a chance in hell. The solenoid's melted. God *damn* it."

—〰—

Just bits and pieces of memory after that, wailing little flashes.

*9:08 PM*
The house was like a dripping mausoleum.

*10:15 PM*
Uncle Jim with a bottle of scotch, trying drunkenly to involve everybody in a poker game. Howard glued to the window, watching the light on Higgins' pier until it finally went out in the raging murk. Aunt Lila giggling strangely as she took a dark green pill with a glass of wine. Flickering shadows, smell of coal oil lamps, wind howling and tearing at the roof.

*1:39 AM*
Wesley's legs dangling off the poker table. Something suddenly touched his toe in the dark. He yanked up his knees and held a candle over the edge. There was a book about sea snakes and Wesley imagined them twisting through the bilge around the furniture legs. But it was just a vodka bottle, nodding loosely in eight inches of water.

*3:20 AM*
Lightning lit up a derelict shrimp boat with windows bashed out, adrift right outside the house. Uncle Jim snoring on the

couch, Aunt Lila in the bedroom. Radio dead. Twisting the batteries like Uncle Jim did to see if he could make them work again. Fingers in the ears so long they hurt, trying to stop the wind shriek. Last candle burning down.

*4:48 AM*

Wesley felt his face start to pinch up with crying. With all the courage he had left, he took the sputtering candle, slipped his feet into the cold, black water and sloshed fearfully over to the sodden sofa where his uncle lay snoring, the rancid stink of used booze mixing sourly with the salt and the mold and the fish.

*6:18 AM*

Howard and Wesley jammed into the second pantry shelf, Howard's face with screaming eyes when the roof grunted, screeched, and flew away into the gray gulf of dawn.

*San Leon, Texas, September 23, 1957 (UPI)*

*Two young boys were found safe today in the debris of their uncle's house here in the wake of Hurricane Denise.*

*The boys, ten year old twin brothers Howard and Wesley Booth, had been left to visit with their uncle and aunt on Thursday while their mother attended a sales convention in Houston, unaware of the intensity of the approaching storm. They appeared shaken but none the worse for wear, telling reporters how they had climbed onto the upper shelf of a closet as the water had started rising and stayed there even as* the roof of the house was torn off by one of the tornadoes spawned by the killer storm. "You could feel it shaking in the dark," said one.

"It's a miracle," said their mother, Mrs. Thelma Booth of Alexandria, La. "But I knew Jesus would deliver them. I prayed for them for two days straight."

Their uncle, James Dunmyer, died in the storm, drowned as the water level climbed to over six feet inside the house. The search continues for their aunt, Lila Dunmyer, but officials offer little hope for her survival.

"This is the worst storm I've ever seen," said E.J. Wolfe, one of the Sheriff's deputies coordinating the search in this area. "We've got over twenty people reported missing. And that's just reported. I hate to think what it's going to add up to when it's all over. These boys were just plain double lucky, that's all I've got to say."

The twins, who had lost their father to a heart attack only a few months ago, seemed to look forward to a period of calm.

"I'll be glad to get back to Louisiana," said one of the boys. "The weather's a lot better than here."

_two_
___

# _dinner_

**B**ooth turned the wheel into the parking lot next to the Flame Club on Lee Street, rain dripping from the trees and windshield wipers thumping. Out of the car, crutching slowly in the slackening rain, headband back in place, he tossed away his last beer can and formed a light tune with the lips for the sake of civility.

Hunching on the crutches past these weeds growing up next to the wall, stucco crumbling damply away and chicken wire bulging out. Look up to see the leading edge of another cumulonimbus canopy slide grayly over the roofline.

A gust of wind puffed the hair up from Booth's shoulders, showing his ears. There was a dank smell here, a black patch of algae on the buckled sidewalk, nourished by the eternal drool of condensate from an air conditioner that drooped and wheezed from a rusting mount. Carefully, then, to avoid a slip. Might unfortunately fracture a bone just before reaching the door of opportunity. Through this red door and into the cool, a jukebox sound of Johnny Winter's *Rock and Roll, Hoochie Koo* over the mull of voices and smoke. That smell of dried beer and pickled eggs, Slim Jims and ashtrays, the *ding* of pinball and click of shuffleboard pucks on powdered wax.

A shout from the bar: "Booth, bring your ass over here!" Eric Simmond's blond hair waving, a blue bow tie bobbing askew under his Adam's apple.

"Eric...Hey, man." Booth goes over, slumps onto a stool.

"What's wrong with your eyes, my boy? They're all red."

"My eyes? Oh...just allergies, man. They're killing me."

Eric reaches over and plucks Booth's hospital badge, still hanging on his shirt. His eyes squinted to read, then he looked up, revelation dawning. "You went to see Howard today, didn't you?"

A fugitive sigh. "Yeah, I dropped by while ago."

"Oh, man." Eric pulled out a box of Marlboros and scraped off the cellophane with a thumbnail. He looked briefly out the window. "What's the situation? Any better?"

"You know, I think maybe there's some improvement. Maybe even some signs of affection. He humped my leg."

"Booth, man, you don't need to say shit like that for my sake." Rather an offended inflection.

Booth's gaze broke away to discover that his elbow was soaked. "This bar is a mess, Eric." Ashtrays gray with mounds of butts, a sodden Budweiser label in a pool of beer. Booth raised a hand to signal for service. "The least we can expect here is a little tidiness."

Eric squinted at him for a moment, then sighed. "Yeah, really. Rudy's being a pain in the ass just like he always is when Archibald lets him run the place. Got the Dubrocs in here sucking up on the free draft, too. A good sixty points worth of IQ between the two of them. Maybe eighty, if you include Rudy." Rudy's attention was diverted by the examination of a switchblade belonging to one of the Dubrocs. Eric's hand reached slyly over the bar to seize a pitcher and fill it from the tap. He slid it in front of Booth, along with a mug. "What's good for the goose is good for the gander, right?"

"Indeed. Thanks, man." He pauses. "Say, you haven't heard anything from Gary, have you?" Booth emptied the mug, refilled it, drained it again.

"Oh, hey, didn't I tell you? They're in town tomorrow night. Out at the Fiesta. You haven't heard them lately, have you?"

"Not since I got back. Saw them on my last leave. Last summer, I guess."

"They're better now, really tight. You know they've been playing the Rainbow over in Houston for the last couple of months, right? Call themselves Holy Thunder now."

"Hmmm...who's Gary got playing lead for him now?"

"Some guy from Lafayette. Andy, something like that."

"Any good?"

"Oh, yeah. I saw them over in Houston a month or so ago. He's good, but he's not as good as you." Eric sipped his beer, then gave a wry smile. "What you thinking about, Booth? Getting back in?"

"Just a passing thought."

"You know Gary was pretty pissed about that thing up in Monroe, man."

"That was a long time ago, Eric..."

"I thought it was pretty funny, myself, but Gary takes that shit seriously. He's got a long memory, Booth." Eric shook a

Marlboro out of the box. "Look, I wasn't sure whether to tell you this or not, 'cause I thought it might start some shit, but Gary told me something else." A pop as he scratched a match into flame. Then the whole matchbook flared ablaze.

"Shit." Eric's hand shook the blossom of fire, dropped it on the floor. Stomping with his shiny black shoes, a round of applause from the others, small embers fizzling in the dark.

"Yeah?" Booth squinting to hear over the jukebox.

"Yeah, what?" A blank stare.

"Yeah what the fuck else did Gary say?"

"Oh, yeah. Well, I guess this guy Andy is quitting. I'm not sure why, but Gary said they're looking for a replacement." Mick Jagger faded off the jukebox. *Paint it, paint it, paint it...Paint it black.*

"Hmmm." Booth rubbing his chin.

"I can see what you're thinking, my boy. All I can say is it might not be as easy as you think."

"Nothing's ever as easy as you think, Eric. But I think Gary might listen to a little reason, don't you?" Booth emptied the pitcher into his mug, tilted to avoid wasteful froth. "After all, what's the best band Gary was ever in?"

"The Remains, man. Who else?" Eric studied his watch. "I oughta go, Booth. Cheryl's gonna have my ass." A rueful pause. "Man, how come we're not still playing? You and me, I mean. That's all I ever wanted to do, you know? And here I am, two kids and a wife, composing bathroom ads."

"We all need bathrooms, man. Hey, you ever want to get together and make some racket, give me a call."

"Cheryl'd shit. The drums are just stacked up in the closet, along with the crap she's saving for the Salvation Army."

"Nothing wrong with salvation, Eric. We could all use a little of that at times, too. I know I could." He spun the empty pitcher into a wobble on the bar, his brow wrinkling. "Is there some reason we're not being attended to here, Eric? Are we hobos, after all?" Booth's hand decisively into the air. Rudy, the bartender, approached with an annoyingly casual waddle.

"Rudy, how about a pitcher of beer for me and Eric here?"

Rudy set his elbows down on the bar, fists pushing up his fat, stubbled cheeks. His hair was combed greasily over his ear, a lazy look of dominance in his eye.

"Booth. I was just thinking about you. We need to talk, pardner."

"Talk?" Booth studied his face. "Sure. How about a pitcher for me and Eric first, and then we'll get down to business."

"That's just what we need to talk about, pardner, is business. The old man says you got to pay your tab."

Booth stared at him with affronted eyes. "No problem. I'll settle up with him just as soon as he comes in."

"He's not here today."

"Well, it'll just have to wait until he gets back, then, won't it?"

"Not really, sport. He told me to take care of it."

Booth looked at Eric. "Is it just me, or does this sound like some kind of ultimatum?"

"Yeah, what's the deal here, Rudy? You gonna hard-ass us about a few beers?"

"A few beers? Booth thinks this place is his own goddamn beer titty." He turned to Booth. "Why don't I go back to the office there and we'll just see how much that tab's up to now."

"I said I'd take care of it when Archibald gets back."

"Well it's cash tonight, then, by God. I know that much." He glanced with a smirk at the Dubrocs down the bar. "Fuckin' place is turnin' into some kinda hippie heaven. Pretty soon we'll have a buncha welfare niggers comin' in to drink with Booth and his friends."

Booth rises from his stool. "*You inbred little fuck...*" But Eric intercedes. "Easy, man, we don't need this shit..."

Booth waved his mother's twenty dollar bill over the bar. "See, here's your cash, Rudy. I think we'll take our business over to the West End, someplace where it's welcome. Say hello to your snuffling little brood for us." Eric guided Booth with his shoulder toward the front door, the Dubrocs turning with pocked, threatening faces to see them out.

Rudy makes a final statement. "Shit. Just carry your ass, Booth. The old man don't need your shit nohow. Simmonds, you're welcome back anytime. I got no problem with you, hear?"

Outside the bar, Eric denounced the lowbrow redneck scum that Archibald hired to run his bar. Standing amongst puddles in the grass, grass tickling the tops of Booth's feet, his chilled glasses fogged over in the afterbreath of the rain.

"Looked like you were gonna go for his throat there for a minute, man."

Booth wiped the glasses with his shirttail. "Eric, can you meet me back here tonight? I've got a little plan."

Eric shifting nervously. "A plan? I don't think so, Booth. Last time, Cheryl..."

"Tell Cheryl it's vital. In the parking lot, OK? Won't take but a few minutes and I guarantee safety. In fact, don't even meet me. Just pop in anytime before like, eight, drink a beer and go take a piss. The only thing I ask is that you unlock the back door while you're back there. It's always unlocked anyway, but just be sure. Rudy won't be able to see you from the bar. Can you do that?"

Booth and his mother stood with Evelyn Bachmeier in her foyer with blinding lights and flashing mirrors. Booth inspected his reflection, fresh new shirt and an indentured smile worth seven hundred dollars on his craven lips. His crutches left at home under the premise of mild exercise.

Inside, Evelyn asks how have you been? And veiled her dislike of Booth's hair with a light comment about the chance of it winding up in the food. Thank goodness for the air conditioning to dry my scalp. Some people live here in this soup and yet never seem to sweat. I have it dripping constantly off my brow, giving the false impression of toil.

"Wesley, it's been so long since we've seen you," Evelyn's arms around my neck, smell the powder and perfume.

But who's this? A girl, standing at the sink. She looks up as they come in, grabbing a towel as she spots Booth.

"Thelma," says Evelyn, "this is Jeri, my niece. She's visiting over from Montgomery. And this is Wesley."

Booth takes Jeri's hand, holding the breath, careful of breathing out fumes from that half bottle of Tokay. But in perfect control just the same. Murmurs, "*Enchanté*." My mother clearing her throat.

Evelyn leading the way inside to the sunken living room. See these ferns and ivy, a glowing cubic tank with triangular fish gliding past a thread of bubbles.

"I thought we'd come in here for a glass of wine before dinner." Booth sitting on the couch next to the fish tank, Jeri settling down at the other end. Crossing her legs demurely as her aunt decants a fine Chablis.

Evelyn hands a glass to Booth, which he declines, strategically. Now an opening gambit from Evelyn:

"I hear you've taken a position with Bob Malone."

"Do you mean with respect to him personally?"

"With his company, I mean."

"Well, not actually. I will be discussing that possibility with him tomorrow, though. I think he wants me to look at something in management..."

"He's applying for a job as a route man. Stocking shelves." Mrs. Booth's voice, interjecting clearly.

"A route man?" Evelyn beaming with a rather superior glint in her eye. "Well, that sounds like a fine place to start. I'd think a smart boy like you'll be able to work your way right on up. Or is this just to save up some money for college in the fall?"

"Well, to tell you the truth, I'd sort of like to keep my options open, career-wise..."

His mother again:

"He told me today he's thinking about getting back in his old band."

Jeri twisted around toward him. "Really? Evelyn told me you're a musician." Her attentive expression. She's not bad, really. The forehead a little high, and with plain glasses, but eagerness always earns bonus points, in my sly manner of speaking. Booth's eyes drawn to the edge of her skirt, just above the knees.

"That's right, but I've been gone for a while. I got drafted and the drummer got married. But Gary, he was sort of the leader, is still playing with another couple of guys. They've been over in Houston for the last few months. Got a new name now…Holy Thunder."

Jeri's eyes widening. "Really? That's the same band that played our spring dance in Montgomery. They're good."

Evelyn clucked at Booth's mother. "Thelma, let's go fix that salad. I think these two can fend for themselves." They stepped up the two steps and away to the kitchen.

Jeri crossed to the stereo. "I just got this new Allman Brothers album. Have you heard it yet?" An innocent appeal in the way she stripped the cellophane from the album, *At Fillmore East.* "It's live."

Booth moves casually over to the liquor cabinet, picks up a bottle, puts it back down. Credibility, second only to the appearance of sincerity. "Put it on, why don't you." His eyes sliding up her leg with some intent. "Are you in town for a while, Jeri?"

"I think maybe I have a job here. My uncle runs the Massey Ferguson place here, and they need a bookkeeper." A compiler of accounts. Promissory notes and collections. I always worry about record-keeping, just as a general observation.

"Well, there's always a need for agriculture, and for agricultural equipment. You'll be an essential link in the food chain, ha ha."

At the dinner table, there was some more throat-clearing by Booth's mother when Evelyn passed him the wine bottle. But a satisfied smile when he refused it.

"Say, Jeri. Want to go for a little ride after dinner? I was wondering if you've heard about that new statue they're building next to the convention center. If my mother will let us use her car for a little bit."

"Well, sure. Why not?"

—◆—

Booth parks his mother's car around the corner from the Flame Club and turns to Jeri.

"This won't take but a minute. I've just got to drop off some papers at a friend's house. Right around the corner."

"How come you parked way around here?"

"They've had a little trouble with vandalism on his street." Reaches under the seat for a stashed bottle of Tokay. "Don't worry, you'll be perfectly safe here. Back in just a shake."

Booth sneaking, bottle of wine in one hand, a penlight from the glove box in the other, between the two cars remaining behind the Flame, one of which was Rudy's chapstick-tan '65 Chrysler. Quietly to the back door past these garbage cans full of beer bottles. He checked for resistance, then opened the door carefully, ready to flee at the slightest sign or squeak. But the door was unlocked, Eric's guerrilla mission accomplished.

Now inside the office, checking the inside door, his eye peeking into the bar where Rudy was playing *boureé* with the Dubrocs under a single hanging fixture. With the penlight he looked around the cluttered desktop, moving papers and vouchers silently. Opening several drawers, finally finding the stack of tabs, with his ominously on top. Fifty-one dollars and some change, an account receivable. Removing his and, cleverly, several more as a smokescreen, so as not to have the finger pointed immediately in his direction.

What else, now? Look around a little, finding a beer invoice with Rudy's elementary signature on the bottom.

Suddenly a better idea. He replaced all the tabs and located a ballpoint pen. Placing his tab on the desktop, penlight in his teeth, he wrote:

*Paid with cash.*

*Rudy Aycock*

He held the beer invoice and the tab up close to the light and compared the signatures. Not perfect, but good enough to cook Rudy's plump little goose. He looked at the others as a guide to form and added yesterday's date and his own signature, using a different pen. The tab back on the stack now in its innocent position.

To the office door again, eye straining through the crack. Rudy and the others still intent on the game, safe in their brainless world. Booth moving like the ghost of an Indian, seeping silently out the back door with mission accomplished. Foot touching the gravel.

Suddenly his belt loop was snagged precisely by the ragged edge of a garbage can lid. An abrupt screeching terror and the cascading crash of bottles in the darkness. For God's unmerciful sake.

To his heels madly, the lid still hooked to his side like a deranged flounder. Through the parking lot and down the street. He issued a panting shriek, finally shedding the lid with a panicked effort and a rip. It clattered clangorously under a nearby pickup truck. Around the corner and to the car, his long arm stretching like Ichabod Crane for the door handle.

Locked.

There's Jeri inside, purse in her lap, mirror twisted around, applying lipstick with the dome light on.

*"Open the door for Christ's sake."* His strangled, pop-eyed whisper, knuckles knocking on the glass. Jeri stretching, fumbling,

her efforts at the lock opposing his. Ear straining toward the bar, hear faint sounds of pursuit, a voice, bottles scattering on the gravel. Finally the door open and Booth into the car, hand at the switch.

*"Where's the fucking key?"*

The sound of jangling. Booth wrenched the mirror violently back into place, staring into it with hunted eyes.

*"Hurry up, God damn it."*

Jeri shrinking away, holding out the keys. "What's wrong, what's the matter?" Her eyes wide open with fear, the lipstick held up like a bullet or a wand.

Booth twists the key. A squeal of fanbelt, and the Biscayne peeling away from the curb. Booth looks back over his shoulder. No sign yet of anyone to witness against him. Weaving quickly through the back streets to evade, lights off and navigating by the glow of porch lights. Jeri again with her questions.

"What in the world...what was all that noise?"

"It was a dog, Jeri. A huge dog. Some kind of wolfhound. I've never seen anything like it. Came out of nowhere. I was just an inch in front of him." He showed her his ripped belt loop.

"See, the thing actually got to me."

"My God. Are you hurt?"

"No, I managed to get my hands around its neck. Felt something snap." He patted around on the seat between them. "Where the heck is that bottle of wine?"

"You took it with you, didn't you?"

*"Shit!"* Still sitting on the file cabinet, Boothprints all over it. "I don't think they dust for fingerprints anymore, do they? Except maybe in murder cases?"

"Murder? You killed the dog?"

"No, no, I just...oh, never mind. Look, I think we'd better head on home. This dog business really upsets me." He lit a cigarette and took a deep drag. Blows it out in a long, narrow plume. "Sometimes it feels like I'm set upon wherever I turn. Have you ever felt that way? Set upon?"

Jeri sat back with a sigh. "Well, I'm not sure exactly what you mean, but I think anyone could, after a certain number of instances..."

"It's the indignity, Jeri. The strangling indignity. I sometimes think that I'm out of my depth. In fact, I've been told that several times, in no uncertain terms."

"I just don't know what to say, Wesley."

He pulled over in front of the Hocus Pocus, that cruciform wiggle-tail neon wraith gyrating on the sign over the door. "I think I'll just step in here for a moment."

And now there's that hesitant, disapproving expression on her face. I've seen it before, on other faces as well. "Do you really think you need any more to drink?"

Booth dropped his cigarette straight down to *pssst* in the gutter. "Drink? Oh, I see what you mean. No, I need to leave a message for a friend of mine. He works here in the daytime and doesn't have a phone."

Here in this blinding store of clear and green and brown bottles. I'm glad that I have cash with me to pay and also to see a new cashier, with hair slicked flat and sticking out ears. He doesn't know me or that there is a stack of my checks marked NSF for non sufficient funds in his drawer beneath the money. The owner, Mr. Quinn, knows me by sight and whips them out, forcing me to trade valuable cash for my counterfeit little instruments. But safely tonight and therefore treated properly, calling me sir and offering to help.

And back out to the car. A humid taste to the air, which is customary. Feel it on my skin. Opening the door. Jeri sitting there hard against the other side.

"I thought you weren't getting anything else to drink."

He unscrewed the wine cap, bottle still in the bag. "Well, I was thinking it would be a nice present for Evelyn."

"I don't know how you can drink that stuff. It only costs a dollar."

"Actually, you can get a better deal than that, if you know the right people."

"And what is that, Tokay? I'm no wine expert, but I don't think Aunt Evelyn would appreciate Gallo Tokay." She tossed her head with what sounded like a sniff. "Especially already opened..."

I can sense some rigidity here in her tone and her body, which is not beckoning. There's an issue afoot, as usual. Try a gentle probe to find out what:

"Is there something wrong, Jeri? Have I said something out of line?"

"No, I just don't see why you need anything else to drink. I just don't know. We were supposed to be going to see a statue. And now here we are. Drinking and driving. Maybe you should take me home."

"Well, I can see your point. To tell you the truth, a lot of people feel the same way, until they get to know me. The thing is that I've got a hyperactive metabolism..."

"And then there was that thing with the dog. It seems funny that I didn't hear any barking."

"Well, Jeri, they say a barking dog never bites. And you saw my pants, didn't you? It almost sounds like you're questioning my honesty." He pulled away from the curb. "I'll tell you what." Slides the bottle under the seat for the right appearance. "Let's take a ride over by that statue anyway, why don't we? I was just a little freaked out by that danged dog chasing me, that's all. Give me another chance?"

And now, a dying roll of thunder over the woods back of Buhlow Lake and the baser instincts rising up. Unbridled. Knowing where these things always lead, one after another like coins in a funnel. Down that path on slips and slides. With the right music in the background and a certain look in the eye. Jeri's skirt riding up during a move to adjust the radio, revealing.

And just a little later, there is the vision of Jeri's breasts, offered in the dashboard glow of my mother's Biscayne.

While the nighttime thrums and cricks outside these laminated safety glass windows.

Just after midnight, see Booth's eyes looking at a red guitar cradled on a stand in the showcase of Williams Music on Bolton Ave. Standing on the sidewalk in a wash of wet neon light, water gushing from a downspout. A small sign mounted on a small easel:

MANAGER'S SPECIAL! GIBSON LES PAUL W/CASE PLUS
FENDER TWIN REVERB AMPLIFIER ONLY $499!
EXCELLENT CONDITION!

Another ounce of wine swallowed pensively from the green bottle of Tokay.

Now the swish of tires and turn to see a police car cruising by slowly, its searchlight switched on and swiveling to investigate. Booth's hand with the bagged bottle dropping smoothly behind him to conceal. Casually back into the car and slowly away from the curb.

A flare of lightning bloomed across the sky to the east, outlining the trees. Booth sucked down another gulp of wine and pointed the Biscayne back across the river.

"Honey, I think maybe you'd better take me home now."

"Honey?" Booth jumped at the sound of a dreamy voice on the seat next to him. Now the cloying feel of a hand on his arm.

"Oh, Jeri." These little hitches in memory an embarrassing problem. Happen at the worst times. And a terrifying expression of love in her face.

"Of course. We're on our way right now." My tongue making these words slur as though I were drunk. And perhaps I have had a bit too much to drink. He stopped the car in the interest of safety and turned to Jeri. "Would you mind driving? I think..."

Jeri's mouth open and terrified glasses reflecting the glare of headlights. Screeching tires and an angry hornbeep blasting.

Jeri's voice rising with a sudden imperious inflection. *"What are you doing? We're right in the middle of the street! What's wrong with you?"* A torrent of abuse.

A door slamming and a clammy feel on the forehead. Feel a little queasy. His door opened suddenly, causing a tilt in his equilibrium.

Booth turned helplessly and projected a column of vomit toward the street where there was the sound of Jeri screaming.

About her shoes.

A clear voice was heard to override the helpless mayhem of his dreaming.

"Wesley? Are you up yet?" A pause. "Wesley." Knocking loudly. "Remember you're supposed to meet Mr. Malone this morning."

Booth's hand to his head, guilt in his heart. Curled up in wetness and fear. A nocturnal emission, pants around his knees. Rancid breath of used wine, and a reprobate feeling of collapse. Oh me.

But brightly, "Yeah, mom, I'm up. Be out in a second." Please get away from that door. You could be in physical danger.

"I wish you knew how it upsets me when you do things like last night. You could at least call, especially with somebody else involved. What did you expect me to say to Evelyn? She had to give me a ride home."

"You could tell her there was a murder in the family." He put his feet on the floor, a sick pain in his head and a swarm of paramecia pulsing before his eyes. "She'd never question that."

"How can you say such a thing, Wesley? What time in the world did you get Jeri home, anyway?"

Oh, Jeri. A thrilling memory of dome-lit lust, shriveling quickly in the face of hangover. Well, at least I'm almost dressed. He pulled up his pants and opened the door.

"God, Wesley. Are you all right?" Eyebrows arcing at my face. "You're white as a turnip."

"Just a little flu." Bathroom a short step away. "Excuse me just a minute." Stepping quickly, mother bumped aside. Booth couples with the toilet in a violent, heaving intimacy. A pump inside, blowing a foul ballast. Puffing and drooling, his knees on green linoleum. Out with the bad, in with remorse. A big piece stuck in the nostril.

"Good *gosh*, Wesley. What did you *drink* last night?"

Blowing the nose into toilet paper. Some pressure involved.

"Drink?" A look of puzzlement, the knitted brows. "Oh, I see what you mean. No..." he reassured from his supplicant position in front of the toilet, "...I think it was those salmon cakes we had at Evelyn's." He gets up unsteadily, sucks water from the faucet. "You know how I feel about fish."

"Well I don't think it was the fish at all. It smells like liquor to me. And look there in the pot. That stuff you threw up is purple." She paused for breath. "What time did you get Jeri home?"

"Mom, give it a rest. We're grown people, aren't we? Besides, you've been trying to set me up ever since I got back." His hand rummaging through the medicine cabinet. "Where's the Alka Seltzer?" Eyes looking into the depth of his mother's hatred. Snapping his fingers in front of her face.

"Mom, the Alka Seltzer?"

Shakes her head. "I hate it when you're like this, Wesley." Stares with unvarnished loathing. "I just know Howard never acted like this."

"Howard doesn't act like anything, mom." Makes to move past her. "Hey listen, let's take this up later, OK? That guy's going to be waiting on me."

And now into Alma's Coffee Shop in downtown Pineville. A bright place, with clattering noise and customers oblivious to my critical condition. Cheerful checkered curtains and a dismally optimistic air of central Louisiana hospitality.

Malone was easy to spot, suited up for business, crewcut and a narrow tie. A handshake at the ready but his eyes cutting nervously toward Booth's long hair. Booth could see a buttressing of the resolve to do his mother a favor.

"Wes, I'm real pleased to meetcha." A firm grasp, always recommended to those seeking to impress. "I've heard a lot about you."

"What have you heard? Nothing good, I hope. Ha ha." The conventional pleasantries.

"No, no, ha ha ha." He slid backwards into the booth. Opening a briefcase, extracting plastic folders. "Is it Wesley or Wes?"

Smiling the prepared smile, Booth sat down, taking care not to upset anything.

"Wesley, usually..."

"How about some coffee, then, Wes? I think I'll have another cup."

Booth declining, wondering how to get hold of a bloody Mary. Or the waitress. She looks kind and I could use some of that right now. As long as it stops short of familiarity, which breeds contempt. He signaled.

When the waitress was standing there, Booth said, "Could you please bring some more coffee for this gentleman? And, you know, I think, if you could, I'd like a big glass of milk and some crackers."

And now Malone warmed to his task, immediately broaching the subjects of retirement and profit sharing, his scalp a shade of gray. Teeth crooked and stained, a starched yellow shirt with the tie restrained by buttons at the collar. Rather an athletic build, likely a former Marine, or a coach. But enthusiastic about Ozark Distributing, responsible for the health and beauty aids sections of fully half of the variety stores in the Ark-La-Miss area.

"Fully half," Malone fondled the oxymoronic fraction. Booth swallows cracker paste and milk for the burn in his stomach.

"Health and beauty aids," Malone declared. "It's as sure a thing as they is." His eyes were wide with the commercial potential of American hygiene.

What would happen if I suddenly struck him? Out of the blue, see him scrambling backwards, his face turning white in shock, condiments and tableware scattering noisily. Just kidding. My casual thoughts of mayhem here in this cultured air of business and friendship.

"One thing I think you'll really like is that there's no dress code at Ozark." His gaze lingering on my hair or my blistered eyes. "I always wear a tie, myself, but that's just the way I am."

Malone filled in the details of the job. Schedules, routes, the pick-up point.

"Yep, you can go jest as far as you want to with Ozark, Wes. Jest remember that the secret is hustle, jest like anything else. Ozark is a service company, and the way to make it big is simple. All you gotta do is be willing to hump it."

This doesn't sound like the job for me, honestly. I'm not much on hustling or humping in the service of others. Latitude is the goal here, and I'm afraid there's not much room for personal freedom, despite the lack of a dress code. The freedom I'm looking for is where I come and go as I please without the squawking, red-eyed albatross of poverty hanging around my neck. I want to be my own man, Mr. Malone. Can you understand that?

But: "Well, I've always believed strongly in personal initiative, Mr. Malone. In the final analysis I only want to be recognized for my achievements in life."

"Then you've got what it takes, Wes." He paused, an actual flush of emotion on his face. "I'll tell you the truth, when I first saw you, I'll have to admit that I had some concern. With your hair, I mean. No offense intended, and I admit I'm biased. But I try to keep opened minded and that's one thing I'm glad of, 'cause meeting a fella with your kind of gumption just goes to show you." His Adam's apple bobbing enthusiastically, within range of a quick lunge with this fork. Kidding, just kidding. Malone pushes a final paper across the table.

"Here's the way we'll work it, then. Monday, I'd like to take you out for your first day on the route. How about we meet at the pick-up point? Now, that's out on Lee street, right past the vet's place. It's a green warehouse on your left. You'll know you're there when you hear the dogs yapping." He stuck a piece of Juicy Fruit in his mouth and held out a key attached to a rabbit's foot. "In case you get there before me. Just look for the white Ford van. Nine o'clock sound OK to you?"

Finally, Booth out the door with a job, his signature upon a provisional bond of assurance. A stamp of doom in the middle of my forehead. But my last check just about gone and then destitution and abuse.

Monday, then, with Malone in his white delivery van to learn the ropes, and I don't plan to get caught in one.

A delivery van, that is.

Or a rope.

See Booth, the author, ready to write.

His materials are at hand: typewriter, paper, manila envelopes, a roll of address labels, an ink eraser with a brush at the end. A fresh black ribbon. Sitting at his green, formica-topped desk with authorial intent.

He types a few words:

*Nicholas Bragg sat in the white truck, with his elbow out the windoe*

Rolls the paper up to erase the *e*. Eraser rubbing the paper nearly through. Rolling it back into position.

*...He picked up the revolved*

God damn it. An angry twist of the knob and rubbing away the *d*.

*...revolver and brought it up to rest on the top of the sterring whee;*

Booth snatches the paper violently out of the typewriter. Fuck it then, creativity is what matters, not monkey skills. Have some menial type this thing altogether. I'll pay them their five little dollars and well worth it.

He got up and walked to the kitchen in the empty house. His mother was gone shopping for the day with Fran. A throb of guilt in his neck for her cheese and lettuce as he pulled them out for a sandwich.

Mayonnaise spread on white bread, gelatinous orange slabs

of Velveeta, lettuce to make it healthy. Big glass of milk. And a pickle here to make it dill. Reading a story in Reader's Digest about a runaway bus that almost went over a cliff, but was saved. There was a football team aboard and they rocked to each side, on command, to counter the rollover tendencies. Teamwork was the keynote.

I try to stay clear of teamwork, if possible. Something about it that bothers me. There's usually a leader, giving commands, and it's usually not me.

A spell of heat in the air, along with humidity. H and H, hand in sticky hand. The air conditioner breathing salvation into the room. We could use a good ice age here, just anytime now. Might cause a problem with the sugar cane crop, but it's for the common good. Sugar attacks the teeth, and the moral fiber, too. New studies in body chemistry pointing up a problem with yet another common household substance.

Now back to my writing. Manually, in longhand this time, so that I'm not distracted by mechanics. So now I need a pen and a tablet or notebook. And can I find one? No. In this drawer? No. Plenty of rubber bands, though, in case I need to construct a slingshot. Also there's a mousetrap. No problem with self defense here. But not a tablet. Or a pen.

Well, actually, the important thing is that I mounted the effort. That no fruit was borne is not indicative of potential. And potential is the...

*Brrrng.* Damned telephone in my ear like a bee.

Booth answers. "Yellow."

"Booth?"

"Yeppers."

"Hey, it's Eric, man."

"Eric. What's up?"

"What are you doing tonight, my boy?"

Oh, swinging on a vine, or swimming desperately in an estuary, yodeling for my life.

"Not real sure, Eric. Why, anything happening?"

"Well, hey, we're going to go check out Gary at the Fiesta. You remembered they were back in town, huh?"

"Yeah, I was planning to head out there, anyway."

"Oh, hey, I dropped by the Flame this afternoon and there was a real row going on. Archibald was on Rudy like stink on shit."

"Really?" My ears perking up. But maintain the appearance of innocent interest. "What was the deal, Archibald find out about all the beer Rudy gives away while he's gone?"

"I couldn't tell for sure. Henrietta and her crew had the jukebox turned up so loud I couldn't hear. Archibald was waving a stack of receipts or something and Rudy kept pointing to this wine bottle he had." Eric paused. "You wouldn't know anything about this, huh?"

"A wine bottle, huh? How would I know anything about it?" A vision of Rudy's fat jowls, waddling in denial, wagging a half empty bottle of Tokay.

"Yeah, looked like a lot higher class of wine than Archibald would be serving. Anyway, I think he finally fired Rudy's ass..."

"Really?"

"Yeah. Looked like it to me anyway. They went back up in Archibald's office and after a while Rudy came out huffin' and puffin' with his face all red."

"Well, he'll be missed for sure. At least by the Dubrocs."

I think the meek, or perhaps the mad, as long as they maintain the appearance of meekness, might indeed inherit the earth.

—m—

His writing materials placed neatly in place for beginning tomorrow, Booth showered and shaven in preparation for tonight. Good of Eric to call, really. Booth walking through the living room, naked, his member obese and tumescent with just the feel of an empty house.

There's also Eric's thought that I might make a run at Cheryl if I had the chance. And he's right, maybe. He remembers as I do the teetering possibility that she might have wound up with me, anyway. Before I got drafted, that night he and I drank all night on orange flavored vodka and the next day, still awake, a year before they got married, me winding up in a wrestling match like kids on the floor with Cheryl. Still remember that moment when I had her pinned to the rug, clear blue eyes of wuthering promise, a frank look of go ahead kiss me. Me a blithering fool, fading from the chance, for some reason of no consequence. And now I know I could still make it happen if I pushed it just slightly. But there's the fact, or at least the notion, that Eric's a friend and there are certain rules I'll abide by. Unless nobody's looking or I think they're not.

Remember, too, that Eric's father died last year, unbelievably, of thirty-six rattlesnake bites. Into the reeds after a bass lure and fell into a nest of hatchling *Crotalus horridus* vipers, lively and poison. Feel a cold coiling under the collar when you're face down, thrashing in the sedge amongst their shingled scales. And those primal, yellow eyes. They said he got up and ran twenty yards with six inch reptiles flinging off him or teeth hooked in his clothes, dying as he went, until his diaphragm arrested and so did he. What a story Eric had to hear. Makes me shiver.

And think how it would be to suddenly see such a thing here on my couch or gliding sibilant from beneath the piano. A swarm of slither, slender and ghastly in their inscrutable intensity, raising their heads two feet off the floor to show me the white underside, swaying sinuously.

The hair standing up on my neck, and which strategy to use, evade or attack? Likely best to get out of the house, seal up the windows and pipe phosgene or fuming nitric acid in through an opening. Meanwhile watching my ankles in the flowerbeds and fearful that others might drop down on me from the eaves. Shield my eyes from the blaring sun and see the things inside, white and gray with red mouths open, dashing themselves against my windows, wild from the gas and frenzied, traces of venom on the glass. Cobras and kraits, a zoo full of dread. Crazy in my peaceful house, seething in my palsied mind.

Wait two hours, then reenter with a mask, resembling a tapir, to see where they lay, lift them out draped on a stick, assured of the safety that only a deadly gas can provide. Pile them, still squirming convulsively, in a nightmare heap in the front yard.

Booth jogging in place, breathing away this scaly, twisting notion. Whew, and sweat breaking out. Put my face in front of the air conditioner for life. Freeze the sweat balls solid and chip them off with a knife.

Snakes all gone now, undo these knots in my spine.

Wesley backs his mother's car out over gravel and pine straw. A dapple of sunlight through the tall pines and oak trees. Brachiating patterns on my dash, Winston smoke in the air. Up the road slowly with eight dollars in the pocket.

First, a stop at the Hocus Pocus on Lee Street for commodities. It annoys me to run out of commodities in the middle of an evening. Disrupts the flow of things. Often as not it's used by others as an excuse to terminate the party and that's more than annoying. I don't like the end of things or lights out or last calls.

He scanned the store quickly for Quinn, then to the beer cooler. Two bottles of Boone's Farm, a penurious purchase, but thrift is a virtue next to godliness. Or at least in the same range. Setting his purchases on the counter to await service. Very fortunate to have missed Quinn on two consecutive visits. Promotes a proper feeling of good will and parity with my fellows...

"Hello, Booth."

That curdling voice over my shoulder. I'm caught, right in the middle of my breath of relief.

"Oh...Mr. Quinn. Sort of startled me. Have to be a little careful, creeping up on a veteran. I've heard of tragedies occurring..."

"Tragedies, huh? I'll have to remember that." Quinn walked around behind the counter and faced Booth with spectacles and closely cropped skull. An amused smile.

"What can I do for you tonight, Booth?"

Oh, I hate being an object of sport. It's such a demeaning role. Hear my captive sigh. "Just these tonight, I think. And two packs of Winstons."

Quinn plucks the cigarettes out of the rack behind him, rings up the sale just as if I were one of the others. "No big plans, then, huh?"

Now comes the demand for money.

But only this:

"You all be careful out there tonight, Wes. I heard something about rain later." And again that smile.

Booth out the door with a nervous feeling of having been had. Or perhaps Quinn's gone mad, lost his grip due to the weather. It's been known to happen.

Driving coolly in my mother's air conditioned Biscayne, rolling on brick cobbled streets with oak overhead weeping skeins of moss as if in a postcard. Best to receive such a postcard while in Flagstaff or Coeur d'Alene or Nome, mailed by a swamped relative.

Booth coasting to a stop in front of Eric's. Massive tall curb to avoid with the bumpers. Can Cheryl hear this door close? Feel a moist girl thrill in her panties? Shame me, but I can't help my thoughts or feelings. They're just unavoidable as I push the white plastic doorbell button and hear shoes stepping inside on hardwood floor.

Now the door opening and oh those fantastic Cheryl eyes. Looking deep into mine, and do they know what they see here? This is the hard part, keeping my errant desires in the dark while not abandoning them altogether. I see how men can wind up shot dead by friends or husbands.

And that smile, too. "Hi Wesley."

On the road, Cheryl leans forward and puts her hand on Booth's shoulder. "How's your writing going, Wesley? Eric said you're writing a novel?"

"Well, just a story, really."

"What's it about?"

"Oh, it's just about the weather...children in peril, that sort of thing."

## *three*

# *booth does the right thing*

Arriving now at the Fiesta Club with a crunch of gravel in the distant reaches of the parking lot. All these cars: Rancheros, Corvairs, Newports, Malibus, Satellites, fourteen VW bugs, seven VW buses, three Renault Dauphines, a bugeyed Austin-Healy Sprite, a host of Chargers, Galaxies, Road-Runners, Barracudas, Javelins, Valiants and jacked-up Camaros. A sea of dewy windshields and sweaty rooftops. And hear that V-8 sound of Saturday night, dust cloud expanding in the headlights.

At the door, Eric paying for all three admissions and edge safely past this crowd of cowboys with their hats, leering in their rude and incidental way.

Eric and Booth up to the bar. Booth buys three beers with his last dollar and a nickel, drinks half of one immediately. Long fingers gripping the other two like talons, thumbs hooked over the rungs of his crutches.

"Man. Looks like they packed the place. But I talked to Gary and he's keeping a table open for us." Eric clearing a way through the crowd for wounded Booth, veteran hero from Fort Meade with combat lies of risk and glory. They eased into the dance floor crush.

Two hundred people, most of them drunk by this hour, in this dark arena of a dance hall, the air compressed with the sound of Led Zeppelin. Menace and wild laughter, this booming in my soul. These tables and chairs made of real wood, sound and deadly in the event violence breaks out, and often it does. Collections of beer cans and glasses of liquor and ice, ashtrays heaped and wet with butts. We could use a waitress here, please. Five air conditioners on each side gasping vapor into the jungle air.

And that Zeppelin, the guitar lead erupting from the amplifier like a ribbon of steel, torn blue-hot from the carbide bit of a Cincinnati lathe.

A half-familiar face looming here in the mob as the song ends. "Booth!" Shaking my hand. "When did you get back?" My puzzled look, grasping for a name.

"Marvin West. From school, remember? I used to live on the east side of town. Marvin West, from the East, ha ha."

"Oh, yeah. Marvin." They find me in spite of precautions. "How's it going?" See Marvin's hair neatly covering the top of his ears. The sound of the guitars checking tunings between songs and Gary's voice announcing.

Marvin continues. "Great, just great." He pulled a fat girl with crossed eyes up to his side. "I don't think you've met my wife, have you?"

"Uh, no, I..."

"Well this is June." He squeezed her proudly.

"Far out. Hello June."

"Well, I'm doing pretty good now. Working for my old man down at the Chrysler place. How about you, Wes? Nailed down a job yet?"

Gloom thrust innocently into my face. Monday and Malone only two days away if I fail in this mission. A life of satisfaction in front of me, seeing to the toiletry needs of old men and the infirm. Drag Malone in here by the ears, change his life for good. A Christian act. Set him up with a bottle of Seagram's, send him out on the dance floor. See him bucking and humping in a corrupted boogaloo with June, his crewcut bobbing amongst the longhairs. Later a drunken fight, Malone squaring off with Marvin out in the parking lot.

"Yeah, you could say I've been nailed, alright...uh, look, Marvin, I've gotta head on up this way. Nice to meet you, June." Taking her by the hand, feel her respond with a surprising, sweaty squeeze, hand of the heart or possibly hormone.

Up front, elevated in a chrome jungle of mike stands and curly creepers of guitar leads, Holy Thunder, lit up in the murk like moths around a gas lantern. Hair to the shoulders, cigarettes dangling, shades even in this darkest of dives. Ovate Zildjian cymbals like gold saucers over the pearl white double bass set of Ludwigs. Magnum speakers blowing the fabric out of big Fender and Marshall amplifiers, cans of beer lining the top. See Gary with his red hair wild and stringy with sweat, singing that song into the microphone.

Booth peeling away, over to the wall slyly so as not to be seen. Stand here and watch the music rave over the pulse and surge of the crowd. My swollen heart, stolen and stomped. But fix my features now and crutch out bravely to the center of the floor, right in front of the band.

Booth standing serenely against the gusts of music. Raising his arms, a beer in each hand, an afflicted, boozing crucifix. Finally Gary's attention surfaced from his involvement with the song to notice the crackpot standing there, the way one looks at the demented or a beggar. A second or so before recognition. Then an uneasy smile and a flourish of stage presence.

Mark the occasion of my return with ambivalence. And a narrowing of the eyes.

Outside, at break time, Booth's crutches make sounds in the gravel. Gary in the safety of a shadow, lighting up a joint. Holding it out for Booth. "Well, how's it been, Booth?" His neutral gaze. "You're hippin' and hoppin'."

Booth declining the joint. "Yeah, really, just a little shrapnel...hey Gary, you all sound good, now, real good."

"Yeah, well thanks, Booth. It took a lot of work to get it that way."

"That was a real nice touch on that *Black Oak* thing. Really smooth."

"Thanks again, man."

Booth lit a cigarette. "Wouldn't be having any use for a good lead man, would you?" His plea sudden and irretrievable in the air.

"Lead man?" A pinch of something on Gary's innocent brows. "What for? We've got one."

"Oh, just wondering. I heard something about ya'll were going to be looking for another guitar."

"Why would we do that? I think we're doing pretty good just like we are. You just said so yourself, right?" A certain set to his jaw.

"Eric gave me the word about your lead guy."

"Oh...that." He looked away with a squint to see if he heard a sound. "That's just a lot of talk. Andy's talking to some people out in L.A., that's all. You know how Eric flaps his jaws." He took a hit on the joint. "Why, you been playing any?"

"Oh, yeah, I been stroking on it. And I still know all the old stuff."

"Yeah? We don't do much of the old stuff anymore."

Booth taking a small sip of beer. "All the same shit to me, man. Just rock and roll, right?"

Gary busied himself with the chain around his neck.

"Reckon you could give me a shot, man?" Booth looked across the parking lot at his fleeting chances.

Gary pinched out the ember of the joint and dropped the roach in his shirt pocket. His gaze slid up to meet Booth's nervous eyes.

"I don't think so, Booth. No hard feelings, man. It just don't feel right, you know?"

My life of slamming doors and denial of the simplest opportunity. Allegiance breached by circumstance, but breached nonetheless. Why do I feel that I might actually choke from this God damned knot in my throat? Try one last thing, and I hate the breathless sound to my voice.

"It won't be like it was before, man." He raised a solemn hand. "I swear on the life of my mother's green and yellow bird."

"Ain't nothing like it was before, Booth." Gary assumed an aggressive stance. "We make five hundred bucks a night and we're talking to a cat from Capitol about a contract to cut some original shit. The big deal, though, is this thing out in Reno."

"Reno?"

"Eric didn't tell you about that, too? Well, it looks like we've got a two week gig at Harrah's opening for Three Dog and some other guys. This could be the real deal. Serious shit. Anybody misses a practice or shows up drunk, they get fired."

"You always were a hardass, Gary..."

"I'm not shittin', Booth. If I was to put in the word and we take you on, my ass is on the line. We're in it for the bread, now. All that other shit's done with..." He paused. "Hey, man, I don't mean to sound like an asshole, but I still remember that time up in Monroe."

"I figured that would have to come up. Look, man, I got no real excuses. In my defense, though, I had just got my draft notice...I sorta got out of hand."

"Yeah, I guess you could say that. Took a piss in the back of the juke box. Four hundred people in the place and Booth's got to whip it out and piss in the fucking juke box."

"It caused a tingling sensation, as I recall..."

"It caused us to get fired, that's what."

"Well, not technically, from what I've been told."

"You're right. That just got the ball rolling. The icing on the cake was when you grabbed the owner's wife by the snatch..."

"She seemed like such a lonely thing. I was just trying to make her feel wanted."

"Her husband was a fucking *Mafia* boss! All those friends of his were packing guns, for Christ's sake. We were lucky we just got fired." A faint smile on Gary's lips in spite of himself. He took a breath.

"Man, Booth, I don't know what it is with you. I mean I never heard anybody play that thing the way you can. Hendrix, Clapton, those guys, but not out here in the world. The thing that really fucks me up is you don't even have to try. Just pick it up and do it—and with a beat-to-shit Silvertone, too. But then there's that other shit, the other side of it. People start partying, you can't just smoke a joint and relax, you gotta start drinking and the next thing you know you're wandering around speaking in tongues or some shit, acting like some kind of fucking mental case..." Gary stopped, a nervous flash in his eyes.

"Hey, I'm sorry, man...just get to talking, you know?" He turned away, then back, wary eyes on Booth's face. "How's Howard doing, anyway?"

"Just about the same, Gary." Seeing an opening and taking it. "How about it, then? Put in a word for me?"

"Here's how it is, then. For old time's sake, Booth. We're holding tryouts right here this Wednesday, five o'clock. I don't know who all's showing up, but I'd say you stand a chance."

Oh, my gladdened heart and clicking heels. Mr. Malone will be disappointed, of course, but...

"Thanks, man. I won't let you down. No shit."

"It ain't a matter of letting me down, Booth. Like I said, you're the best I know, and that's the way to make bread. And I ain't promising anything. Let's just see how the tryouts go, huh? Hey, look, I gotta split, man. See you Wednesday...Oh," He turned back. "You got your own rig, right?"

"Uh, sure. Why?"

"Well, I still remember that raggedy ass guitar and you always borrowing an amp..."

"Don't worry, man. I've had a few investments pay off lately. See you on Wednesday."

Now it's Monday and there's Malone, waiting next to the van in front of the green warehouse on Lee street, under the oaks with a cigarette, one hand in the pocket of gray slacks.

Booth was twenty-two minutes late but ready with a story of delay by reason of carburetor trouble, some convenient grime from the door latch smeared on his hands to prove it. Credibility is everything, I've heard it said, and I believe that it's true. Credibility and a forthright attitude.

"No problem, Wes." Malone poured the remainder of his coffee from the red plastic Thermos cap onto the ground, a black bolt splattering dust and oak leaves. Screws the cap back onto the bottle. "We're just gonna take it easy today. Sorta just get used to the routine."

Routine is another word that will make my flesh creep. Please don't use that one again.

"Yeah, once you settle into the routine, I think you'll get just real comfortable with Ozark."

And on the road. These plastic crates rattling in the back of the van, so loud that shouting is necessary. A clipboard with an order form on the console between the seats. Likely these things could wait and not bring about the collapse of the world economy. A face of irreproachable enthusiasm nevertheless, throb of dread in the soul.

Half an hour later Malone parks the van in front of the H&L Variety store in downtown Pollock. A false wooden front and large picture windows. Opening the back doors of the van in full view of passersby and gathering the tools of the trade, as horribly menial as I expected. A clipboard, a price gun, and, most ominously, a feather duster. Malone directs Booth to bring a stack of crates inside, using the hand truck.

Inside, a smell of ointment, leather, and the oil and creak of wooden floors. A rural assortment of garments, stacked or hanging. And a rotisserie of nails in bins, with a scoop like the bill of a tin pelican to dump them into the scale nearby. Malone introduces Booth to the proprietress:

"Miz Williams, this is Wesley Booth. He's going to be taking over the route starting next week. We're just getting him started today." Donning his apron with the strap tied in back. A grin now to encompass and encourage a good-natured acceptance of my long hair. "I know he looks like a hippie, but Wes is gonna be OK. I think he's gonna fit in real fine. I know his mama, and you just won't find a finer woman." Booth's smile of warmth and goodness at heart hurt his face, but the right appearance is worth a thousand lies. It rounded out the picture of one eager to fit in. I may be a square peg, but I can fit the geometry of any hole you throw me at. As long as I can squeeze my way in. I'm a simple little plastic man, like Gumby.

Now back to the health and beauty aids section. Products scattered and mixed indiscriminately. The disorder could cause a serious misunderstanding, at the very least, amongst the bumpkinry. A box of Massengill broken and expanding, dampened by a pool of hydrogen peroxide. Malone reached into one of the crates and stood up flapping a red cloth article.

"I went ahead and ordered you an apron. The company likes you to wear one." Feel sweat behind my ear and a worm in my gut. This intolerable affront, wrapped in an apron and hustling around with a feather bouquet blooming from my pocket. But just hang on until Wednesday.

Malone raising a roguish eyebrow. "Between you and me, I think it's to protect them in case you spill something or get ink

on your clothes. So they won't have to buy you some new ones."
A chuckle at this notion of petty corporate chicanery.

Malone set about the repair in a businesslike fashion, show-ing how effortlessly it could be accomplished. In a moment he looked up and pointed. "Tell you what. I'll take care of all this stuff on this end. You get started down there with the Kotex."

A tapping of typewriters and chunk of adding machines. Monday afternoon at 3 o'clock and Booth sitting with his mother outside the door of J. Winston Prine, manager of Guaranty Bank.

"Bob Malone tells me you're going to work out really well. It was decent of him to help you like this." His mother's veritable blush of pride in this aura of employment and the imminent extending of credit. Attainment always a goal of hers. And mine, too. In fact, I'd say the only way we differ, really, is in our approach. Booth's hair was slicked down with Brylcreem to please his mother and Mr. Prine as well.

"Oh, Wesley. You remember that Fran and I are going to Dallas Wednesday?"

"Dallas?"

"I know I told you. It's that big regional World Book conven-tion. We'll be back on Sunday." She reached over to adjust his collar with a critical eye. "I'm going to stay out at Fran's tonight so we can get all our things packed. Tomorrow, I wonder if you..."

"Uh, could you excuse me a minute, mom? I've got to go to the bathroom before we start signing papers."

Sitting now in this stall, his thing hanging primal and primate, tumescent, the tip just touching the water. Excited by the prospect of money. And the shoes of a financier visible amongst a scattering of newspapers in the next stall. Hear the delicate grunting, a member of the upper crust. It would be a simple thing to reach down with this Zippo and set fire to the daily news. Or perhaps, if one had prepared for it, flip a live snake over the partition. Hear his yelping little cries, the wild struggle to get out, pants around his ankles. Just an idle thought, fanged with the lightest touch of madness.

Back out to his mother and just now the office door opening, Mr. Prine with outstretched hand, his smile of commerce and warmth. "Thelma, it's good to see you. And Wesley. Back from the Army, then. We sure were glad to hear you made it safely." An expression of compassion offered to his mother, the intimate inflection. "How's Howard doing, Thelma?"

"Well, there hasn't been much change, I'm afraid. We keep hoping, of course..."

"And praying. I know we're just Methodists, but we always remember Howard in our prayers." An iron glance at Booth.

"I know you do. We've been blessed with so many friends during this time, Mr. Prine."

Sitting now around this large and heavy desk, Mr. Prine's fingertips touching in front of his chin. "So, let me guess. Wesley has got himself a job and wants to talk about a car loan." His smile for my mother, his eyes for me. "Did I come close?"

Mrs. Booth's subordinate chuckle. "Now aren't you clever."

And talk of interest rates and payment schedules, the pushing of forms and assurances back and forth. Just apply my signature with a flourish here and here and there, and done. Present this check to one of the tellers and out the door with my head at the same level as my peers. Rising to leave, Mr. Prine ushers Booth's mother out. Booth's eyes on the pale blue check still in Prine's hand.

"Wesley, I wonder if I could have just a moment with you alone? It won't take but a minute, Thelma. Just have a seat right over there if you would."

Door closing and Mr. Prine back to his desk. Opening a drawer. "Wesley, it's not my business to interfere in the affairs of my customers...but I want to show you something." Booth stands there waiting to be shown.

Pulling out an envelope and handing it to Booth. A collection of yellow checks. A sudden itching in the ear.

"A Mr. Quinn brought those in here last Friday. Feel free to count, but they add up to just over eighty dollars. I take it you know this Mr Quinn, right?"

"Well, I think..."

"He owns the Hocus Pocus over on Lee Street, just to refresh your memory. The liquor store."

"Ah...yes, I believe..."

"All they sell is liquor there, Wesley. Again, I don't want to meddle, but your mother is an old friend of mine and I've seen her go through a lot these last few years."

"I think I see what you're driving at, Mr. Prine. And I can understand your concern. Actually, as it turns out, the Hocus Pocus is right next to the gas station where I fill up, so I often cash checks there. I'm of course embarrassed to see..."

"Horse shit, Wesley."

"Pardon?" My shocked face.

"Your dear mother might believe it, but I'm not quite as innocent as she is." He handed the check to Booth. "You'll see that I've subtracted the amount of the checks from the loan total, and we'll just keep it between you and me. But I want you to be sure to keep better track of the payments on this loan than you have of your checkbook. I'd take it real personal if your mother got a black mark on her credit because of anything like that."

"Well I can assure you..."

"I'm sure you can, Wesley. But don't. Just put in a day's work for a day's pay and take care of your mother and your brother. Everything else'll fall right into place." Prine shows Booth the door, his lips set in a summary fashion. The door closed in my smiling face. Just a quick scoop of shit, flung to be sure I don't forget my station. I've recently come to know it as a general deluge, dripping from my hair in feculent globs.

But this thin check nevertheless worth six hundred and twenty dollars. Booth takes it immediately to a teller, pockets the cash.

"OK, Mom, you ready?"

"Well, my goodness. What was that all about?"

"Oh... Mr. Prine just wanted to wish me luck on the job. Had a couple of investments he thought I might be interested in."

"Investments?" Looking up over her glasses. "He must have been pulling your leg." Through the bank lobby, afternoon depositors looking at Booth and his mother walking through the hush of finance.

"I didn't get that impression at all, Mom." He opened the tinted glass door into the glaring, liquid heat. "In fact, he said he can see a lot of potential in a man like myself."

It was the next day, a Tuesday, marinating in the basin of a central Louisiana summer.

Hear the feedback shriek and stomp of bass in Booth's closed and frigid room. *Voodoo Chile (Slight Return)*, savage Jimi Hendrix homage to manic passion stuffed into Booth's 12 by 14 foot bedroom. He stopped to get rid of his cigarette, burning its way up to his nose. Hear pounding on the door.

Opening the door to find his mother there, her eyes wide with shock.

*"Wesley, for God's sake turn that thing down! What are you trying to do, wake up the whole world?"* Her outraged voice shrilling in my face.

"The world's already awake, mom. It's daylight, isn't it? And I'd appreciate it if you'd not take the Lord's name in vain..."

"Don't be smart with me right now, Wesley. I put up with too much of this when you were in high school..." Peering around him at the Fender Twin Reverb, hissing black with menace, red light glowing ominously. "Where did you..." Looking up with her disbelieving face. "Did you spend that money on *this*? The money for the *car*?"

"This is a little awkward, Mom. I thought you had gone to Dallas."

"Dallas? I'm not going to Dallas until tomorrow. Is that the car you bought out there? That *thing* in the driveway? I thought somebody was robbing the house when I saw it."

"It's a perfectly good car, Mom. I just saw an opportunity to save a few dollars..."

"Wesley, I could just *kill* you! Perfectly good car. I looked at it. The seats are nothing but wire. Do you mean you actually took that money I signed for and bought this...*stuff*? I can't *believe* ..."

"Mom, you're getting all worked up here..."

"Don't you *dare* talk to me like that, Wesley. I've had all I can stand of this. You lay around here while I work my head off every day..." She paused, momentarily speechless. Then her eyes narrowed, her lips pursed up with gathered fury. "You take every bit of that stuff you bought back and get my money back. And you have got to keep this job. I mean it. I let you go because of Howard and you had such a rough time in the Army, but I'm at my wit's end..."

*BRRRRNG!* His mother staring in rage, actually quivering with it. Booth feigns an attempt to get free of the guitar strap. "Mom, you want to catch that, please? I've got a little problem here."

*BRRRRNG!*

"Mom, the phone."

Finally turning in disgust, stepping to the living room.

"Hello?"

Booth turned off the amplifier, guitar quickly back in the case. Thought for sure she was gone. She said so, didn't she? These unfortunate hitches in timing, throwing me always into conflict. Close this door, then, to hide the source of the trouble. Out of sight, out of mind. Into the living room.

His mother holding out the phone, her gaze of hatred. "It's for you. It's Jeri."

Booth speaking into the mouthpiece, head inclined earnestly. "Yellow."

"Hello, Wesley? This is Jeri. How are you doing?"

"To tell you the truth my neck's acting up. I have a real pain in it."

"Oh. I'm wondering if you're feeling better. It's been a few days, and I thought maybe I'd hear from you."

"What can I do for you, Jeri?" His mother choosing this moment to move the kitchen table scraping across the floor.

"Well, don't you think maybe you owe me an apology?"

"An apology?" Again an annoying noise from the kitchen.

"I mean, you did throw up on my feet."

"What? Listen, Jeri, I'm afraid there's a big mixup here." Booth moving casually to the kitchen door, and his mother's face glaring. "I think I know what might have happened. You know about my twin brother Howard, right?" His mother looking up. "No? Well, I guess nobody thought to mention it, but your aunt can tell you. Anyway, he's the nicest person, but unfortunately he's in an institution. I think he's a little embarrassed about his condition, although he shouldn't be. Anyway, here's the thing. Howard does have the habit of using my name sometimes when they let him out on furlough." Listening again, see his mother's unbelieving expression. "No, I understand. I'd feel that way too. And I'm really sorry. You sound like a nice person. Listen, if you'd like to write to Howard, I can give you his address at the hospital..." Looking at the receiver, then at his mother. "That's funny. She hung up."

His mother picked up a Sunbeam mixer, apparently for use as a weapon. Then, shaking, she put it down. "What kind of person *are* you, Wesley? How could you even *think* of saying something like that?" Her voice a harsh, hopeless whisper.

"Mom, can't you tell when I'm kidding? Good grief. I'm just trying to lighten things up a little..."

"Lighten things up? I just wonder how you can live with yourself sometimes. Saying things like that about Howard."

"Mom, you know I didn't mean it. I just feel we've got to make the best of things."

She looked up and shook her head with streaming eyes. "I swear sometimes I think you've decided to kill me."

"Kill you? What in the world..."

"I do. I think maybe there's something wrong with you and that you might kill me some night."

"Mom, I just don't know what to say..."

"I think that whatever happened to Howard might happen to you, too. Don't you think God could strike you down just like he did poor Howard?" She sobbed again.

"Mom, I..."

"I love you Wesley, more than my life, but I'm afraid of what's going to happen to you if you don't get yourself right."

Late that night, Booth suffered a dream. There was a pool, formed by an estuary, the color of green obsidian under a doomsday sky. At one end of the pool a fish lay on the bottom, fat and pearlescent black, its tail waving slowly and prehistoric eyes watching. Also in the pool, Wesley waded toward the distant side. Just as he started to step up on the bank the fish made it's lunge, a muscular swell on the glassine surface. Wesley made it with a terrified effort and turned back to see. Instead of the fish, he could see the form of a man on the bottom of the pool, face down and drifting. As he leaned closer, Booth could see the detail of a tee shirt with a small hole ripped in the shoulder. A current rolled the man face up in a slow wobble. It was Howard, smiling sweetly. Booth awoke in the air conditioned darkness trying to scream, but making only the helpless sounds of a nursing puppy.

In the morning, see the Les Paul first thing, leaning against the amp, that Freudian shape of rock and roll. Hips and tits, if we stretch the metaphor far enough. He was glad to find that his mother was already gone. A bit of remorse in the spleen for that scene yesterday. No need to have said those things, really. Only breeds more hatred.

But I do wonder why people push me into that frame of mind.

Five o'clock the next afternoon at the Fiesta Club, Holy Thunder holding court, in the literal sense, here to make judgment on a new member. Booth sitting offstage, in a folding steel chair, guitar strap loosely over his shoulder. A cup of coffee next to his boot and cigarette dangling, smoke weaving into his curls as his fingers made shapes and riffs on the pearl inlaid rosewood neck of the Les Paul.

This nervous waiting while the other candidate ripped through *Sunshine of Your Love*, hair styled like the Christ and honey dripping from his fingers. See that exchange of looks between Gary and the bass player, but their gaze just avoiding mine. A gulp of coffee to calm the nerves.

I find myself in an execrable situation here, waiting like a beggar for my rightful position in this group of minstrels. Just a flick of circumstance and I could be calling the tunes instead of Gary. I'll have to say it rankles me just a bit. Not enough to justify anything untoward, of course, but I think you can see my discomfiture.

I mean, I recall those days when we used to load up the stuff in a gray '58 Ford station wagon and head out. Me and Gary and

Wylie and Eric. Drive a hundred miles to Baton Rouge or Shreveport or Monroe, french fries and cigarettes and beer. Pull into a honky tonk parking lot in the late afternoon, craters of mud in the gravel, broken reflections of oak and moss in the brown water. Unload the equipment, everything black—amplifiers, guitar and drum cases, shades, black and chrome. Even black leather gloves worn on the right hand after we saw the Music Machine wear them that night up in Shreveport. Paint it black. Watch your back.

Now Booth's turn, stepping up on the stage. Friendly handclasp with the other, see his Jesus haircut and confident smile.

"Shit." Booth's ankle caught by a cable. Freed helpfully by the competitor. Booth smiles. "Thanks, man." But a quick swing of this Gibson and see him spitting out teeth. Just kidding. These little imaginings pop up.

Gary speaks. "Alright, Booth. Just like old times, right? Check this out...a Les Paul." To the bass player. "Hey, you shoulda seen this thing Booth used to play, man. Some places they'd take one look at it and refuse to let us in." He pointed. "Just plug into that Marshall there. Make you sound like Hendrix, right? What's it gonna be?" Gary's voice breezy, businesslike.

And introducing the others: Malcolm on bass, left-handed like McCartney, thin as a stick and hair parted in the middle. Now Andy. The brotherhood handshake. "Heard a lot about you, man. Gary says you can kick ass." Andy picked his low E string for a tuning reference, Fender Jaguar flashing red and chrome. "Whatcha want to start with?"

Booth's fingers twisting knobs. Points at a CryBaby wah pedal. "How about *Voodoo Chile?* Still do that one?" He stood up and wedged the filter of his Winston under a string on the tuning head.

"*Voodoo Chile?* For a tryout? That's what I call balls, man." Turns to the others. "Ya'll get that?"

That opening riff in muted, quacking scratches, then the main chords, punctuated by trills and slides, the confluence as the rest of them enter the flow. And slide into it, feel the resonance, my thorny soul of quacking passion. Now hear Gary sing those words into the mike while I shape these chords and add these trick little fills.

Oh, this incomparable feel of music, sweet shameless pulse of incandescent lust. I would give away my legs and perhaps a testicle if it guaranteed I could still play the electric guitar. See me roll bravely onto the stage in my wheelchair, audience in awe of my spirit and talent, the women trembling and damp.

Now that hovering breath of tension and into the lead break. Just the right timing and bend the G string halfway across the neck, a moan of feedback, then the demon growl of triple pull-offs on the A string down by the nut, toothed and syncopated and raw, fingers like a marauding spider.

A quick glance at the twerp with Christ hair and his grin wiped off. See him snapping up his case, sitting down to hear the rest with an attitude resembling respect.

When the song was over, Gary came up. "Not bad, Booth, not bad. Why don't you go up front and grab a beer, man? We'll be out in a few minutes." He could hear Andy with his head turned away say "Oh wow," then looks over with a nod of appreciation.

In the front, Booth sat at the bar with a can of Schlitz, watching a man fill the beer kegs with carbon dioxide. Small talk about the weather and the chances of snow this winter. Not many, the man thought. But hopefully just a ghost, so that my throat might warble a small tune of relief from this ungodly heat.

Presently, Gary and the others come out with looks of welcome.

"Looks like you're it, dude."

Gary buying beer to toast and a general air of camaraderie and planning. Speaking of which, Malone will have to be told. Oh, my shiver of unthrottled delight.

"Here's the way we've been doing things. We practice every afternoon before a gig. Who's got the play list so Booth can bone up?" And so on.

See Booth lounging, victorious ale in hand, in the company of comrades, sitting on his rightful stool of wood and vinyl. When he saw Sam, the defeated guitarist, dejectedly hauling his equipment away, Booth magnanimously called him over and gave him a beer. Here but for the grace of God goes Booth. Talk to him with compliments and make him feel better. Actually helping him to the car with his equipment, gushing over his skill and whatnot while the young man looked curiously into his eyes.

Booth goes to the bathroom. Holding it in his hand, he looked out the window into the parking lot and saw that Sam's Falcon was still there. Gary was talking earnestly and somewhat furtively into his face, which was considerably less dejected.

On the way out after the others are gone, Gary takes Booth aside and says these words.

"I'll give you the word, Booth, but keep it to yourself, 'cause it's not on paper yet, OK?" He paused for drama. "We're going to fucking Reno."

"Reno? Oh wow. What's the deal?"

"Fucking-A, oh wow. It's at Harrah's, opening for Three Dog. If this comes through, we're done with nickels and dimes. Can you dig it?"

"Well, I'll need to check with my spiritual advisor, but I think I can dig it. When's this happening?"

"Next couple of weeks. We still got three gigs here in town and that one down in Baton Rouge. But I'm not booking anything after that."

"Far fucking out, man." A gout of sweat runs suddenly down his cheek. Booth diverts it with a quick finger. "I will miss this humidity, though. It's so pleasant this time of year."

Gary takes a sip of beer, flips his red hair off his neck. "You know, that kid Sam's not too bad, huh?"

"Not too bad at all, Gary." Booth assumes the slightly superior air of one wounded. "You offer him the backup spot?"

Gary's eyes quickly up to deny, but then he blew out a breath.

"Tell you something, Booth. I've pretty much got this thing headed the way I want it now. I figured it was gonna be a real setback when Andy got that deal in L.A." He wiped sweat off his forehead with his shirt sleeve. "But then who shows up? Fucking Booth, man, with the same kind of timing you got on that axe. Perfect. Now, I was faced with I think they call it a dilemma. I don't take as many chances as I used to and I had some real mixed feelings about this one, but finally I figured what the fuck, I want a contract, and with the people they got playing now we need somebody heavy on the guitar. So I said OK."

Gary paused and shook out a cigarette. He lit it and looked at Booth through the smoke which moved to the left with an imperceptible waft of air.

"So to answer your question, and to keep things up front,

yeah, I told Sam to keep close to the phone for a while. I hope you can dig it, but I'm covering my ass on this one."

"Well you gotta do what feels right, you know. But you don't need to worry. All I want is a shot at it. Sam's a nice kid, but I'm planning to keep his little Jesus ass unemployed."

—⁊⁊⁊—

A telephone call from Booth in his new position in the scheme of things, albeit on a sort of probation.

"Mr. Malone?"

"Speaking."

"This is Wesley Booth."

"Oh hi, Wes. What can I do for you?"

"I just called up to let you know that I'm not going to be able to accept that job after all."

"What?" A pause. "How come?"

"Well, it turns out that some friends of mine have asked me to join a band." Oh, the giddy sense of joy that quitting always brings. I'm in my element when I'm on my way out.

"A band?" A slightly incredulous inflection. "You mean music?"

"That's what I was doing before the army, Mr. Malone."

"Yes, but..." He paused. "Well, this kind of puts me in a bind." A pause. "You know, it's not for me to say, really, but I'd think you'd be wanting something more substantial, with the situation with your brother and everything."

"Well, I appreciate your concern, but the money's good, and I feel that I have to follow my heart, if you get my meaning."

"OK, then, Wes. But you might want to think a little bit about what a steady paycheck means these days."

Booth hangs up the phone. Malone seems like a decent man. How did he ever get involved in toiletries?

And how did I ever get involved with him?

—⚡︎—

Booth receives a telephone call on the following Saturday, the very afternoon upon which a practice session was scheduled to put a bit of polish on Booth's integration into the band. In preparation for an opening at the new Delta Spur Lounge in Baton Rouge. "A pretty big deal", according to Gary. "They've got seating for like six hundred people."

The call was from his mother.

"Can you please go over to the hospital right now and help the doctors with Howard? They need some help with something they're doing."

"What? Mom, I'm doing something myself right now."

"Well, whatever it is, I know it's not work, so don't fight with me on this, Wesley. I've got to go into a meeting with Duncan and Pru right this second."

"I'm leaving for practice right this second. What the heck do they...?"

*Click.*

"God damn it."

Booth arrives at the hospital, guitar and amp on the back seat of the Rambler. Waits for the doctors in the lobby of Ward D, with his badge pinned on. Presently the doctors arrive and Booth tightens his lips to explain his busy schedule.

"This shouldn't take very long. What we're going to do here, Wesley, is just to move Howard to another room. We think it could play a part in his recovery." They talk in hushed tones, to soothe the mind.

"Really? How's that?" Glancing at the clock.

"Well, it may sound a little odd, but they've done some studies with patients up in...where was it, Hal?" Asking the other.

"Connecticut. New Haven."

"Righto. Anyway, they tried an experiment up there where they altered the patient's surroundings. They reasoned that the same setting might ultimately contribute to the static state of the patient's condition." He smiled. "They were very gratified with the outcome."

"In fact, the results were rather remarkable." The other speaking, his glasses pinched between fingers. "I have to caution against being overly optimistic, but 28 percent of the test patients demonstrated a measurable gain in social cognition. And if I remember correctly, they were able to reduce drug therapy in something like, oh, 35 percent of the cases. After an initial adjustment period, of course."

The first doctor again. "We've asked you here because we want to move Howard over to the Judd Annex. We don't anticipate a problem, but it does require a walk across an open stretch, and given his response to some environmental stimuli, we thought it would be a good idea to have a family member present. It seems to act as a stabilizing influence, generally."

"Well, I'm not sure exactly what you want me to do."

"Oh, we'll take care of the actual restraint, I should say, *control* aspects. We'd just like for you to be there to offer support, sort of hold his hand, so to speak. Not necessarily physically; I think you know what I mean. We don't anticipate any trouble; we've administered a sedative." He paused. "Well, I think we'd better get on with it." He inserted a key into the lock.

The door swung open and see Howard in his chair. The doctors took their places on either side of him and placed their hands gently on his arms, speaking quietly. They raised him to a standing position. As they walked slowly toward the door, a look of anxiety crept into his drugged eyes. His hands clutched at the gown he wore loosely and his humming grew louder. He began to resist the doctors' efforts by leaning backward, his arms forming the shape of an isosceles triangle.

"Wesley, if you will, please."

"What? Do what?"

"Just talk to him. Say anything at all, please."

Booth stepping forward with loathing and guilt. "Hey Howard, man, it's OK. It's just me. Wesley." Howard's eyes came slowly up from the floor.

And Booth could see into them, looking away to avoid the blank marrow of hell that was inside there. But then looking back with an effort.

"It's OK, Howard." Holding out his hand. Howard's eyes locked now on his face. Relaxing a bit and the doctors moving forward with Howard like a wraith in between. Slowly to the door and a pause for the doctors to check for reaction. Walking down the checkered hallway. Booth to the door first, opening it to clear the way.

Once outside, one of the doctors suggested that Booth walk next to Howard. Booth stepped up so as to give the appearance of helpfulness. Grasping the arm, feel the wasted biceps and the unsteadiness. Howard's head turns briefly toward Booth, then back to the front as they shuffled on the sidewalk with flowers around them. I see the flowers and sometimes stop to smell them but just keep walking with the mind turned off.

A strong breeze washed down the canyon between the buildings, causing Howard's gown to flap. There was a tensing of his arm, pulling it back, and his humming grew louder. Suddenly, Booth felt his wrist in the grip of Howard's hand. He started to pull away, but Howard turned slightly and leaned his head against Booth's shoulder.

"What's he doing?" Booth's fearful voice.

"Take a look at this, Hal." Both doctors slightly in front, craning their necks around to see. "What do you think?"

"It's hard to be sure... let's just keep going."

Another fifty feet and they came to the steps of the Judd Annex, a brick building not unlike the others. "First floor. To your right, Wesley. Just down this way." Down this hallway with doors closed and the doctors moving ahead, Booth locked in a macabre step with Howard in his gown. At last a door and Doctor Hal fumbling with a key.

They went inside the room. Bright window with light green curtains open. Doctor Weber separated Howard gently from Booth's arm and sat him down on the bed. "Well, what do you think, Hal? Was that just an aberration or do you think something happened there?"

The two doctors stood looking at Howard in a classical way, Hal holding his glasses pensively. Howard had an introspective look on his face and Booth asked "What's the deal here? Is something going on?"

"Let's just step outside for a moment, OK?" As they stepped out the door, Dr. Weber gave some brief instructions to an orderly.

Once outside the room, Weber said, "Wesley, I don't want to get your hopes up—these things are always so ambivalent—but what just happened might be a good sign for your brother's recovery. For a patient in Howard's condition to respond like that...well, we'll have to do some evaluation, of course, but it may be a sign that he emerged from his shell just a little. We also have a new facility down in New Iberia that might play a role, if it seems to be indicated. We'll see..."

—⁂—

And now Booth hauling his guitar and amp into the Fiesta Club, just 50 minutes late but with a bulletproof alibi firmly in hand. Only a little late, anyway.

The others up on stage, all except Gary, standing idly with cans of beer, plumes of cigarette smoke brilliant in the glare of stage lights. Booth stepping onto the stage and hear the conversation turned off.

Malcolm turning to move over tentatively to where Booth was plugging in his guitar. His look was nervous, his voice almost a whisper.

"Where you been, man? We been waiting for a while."

"Yeah, hey, I'm sorry, Malcolm." He turned up the volume and ran a quick riff down the neck in A harmonic minor. "I had to take care of a thing with my brother over at the hospital. Couldn't be avoided. Where's Gary?" Looking around with righteous eyes, secure and forthright in the innocence of a good deed done.

"He went out to use the phone. You didn't see him on the way in?"

"Must have missed him. I think I'll..." But then Gary steps silently out of the murk and up on the stage.

"Hey, Booth. How's it going, buddy?" Shakes his hand.

"Oh, OK. Listen, sorry to be a little late. I had to go help them move Howard over at the hospital."

"Move him?" Gary looks around at the others.

"You know, to another room there." Booth reaches down, clicks the amp to standby.

"Let's see. We were gonna practice at five, right?" Gary looks at his watch. "Well, shit, it's nearly six. I guess we'll have to call it off." He looks around the stage. "You guys don't mind, do you?"

The other three look at him silently.

"I mean, it looks like Booth is cool with the time thing, so I guess maybe we ought to just say fuck it and blow the thing off. Go get drunk or something instead of wasting our time here."

"Hey, man..." Booth moving forward with an attitude of humility and good will, to explain the situation. "It was Howard, Gary. I had to go help them over at the hospital..."

"Oh?" He steps aside with some drama. "Why don't you tell these guys who Howard is and why it was that they've been standing here, dicks in hand, for the last hour."

"What? I..." Booth, with dumbfounded voice, preparing to talk reason.

"No, really. It'll give Malcolm there something to tell his little girl since he missed her swim class so he'd be here at five." Gary took a glance toward the entrance.

Booth feels a pulse hammering at his windpipe.

Gary takes a step closer, looks into his eyes. "I'm gonna have to ask you to leave, man."

"Leave? Come on, it was Howard this time, no shit. I was just doing what my mom asked me to. What the fuck are you doing, Gary?"

"Just what my mama told me to, Booth. Taking care of business."

"Yeah, but...

"I don't really want to hear anything, man. Just split, right? I'm sorry, seriously, but we've got some work to do." He turned away, as though twisting a crappie off his hook and dropping it back into the slime of a bayou.

Booth can see Malcolm's eyes, and those of the others, looking at him. He unplugged his guitar with a knot in his throat like a bass plug with three hooks.

Now see Booth on his way out, lugging 80 pounds of Twin Reverb and his guitar. Wires dragging on the floor behind him, face straining forward, neck veins bulging. His guitar case, hastily snapped shut, popped open and spilled the Les Paul onto the floor. As he was jamming it back into the case, Sam, the one with Jesus hair that he had defeated in the tryouts, came in. He was using a hand truck to maneuver a Marshall half-stack among the chairs. Sunshine streaming in the doorway, igniting motes in the cigarette smoke. When he saw Booth, he stood back, the way one does to avoid the deranged.

But he had this to say:

"Hey, this is a real bummer, man." His head turned toward the dance floor and then turned back with a certain look. "You know?"

## four

# *mumbo*

Booth squinted grimly through the smoke of a Winston and let the engine wind up. When the moment was right, he punched the **Low** button on the shift panel. The car, his hundred dollar '62 Rambler Ambassador with seats laid open to the wire, slewed sideways with bald tires smoking. Booth hooked his left pinky in the vent frame and stomped the high beam switch. The blaze lit up the pine woods crowding the road. Low tendrils of mist swirled in the car's wake. Roadside wildlife ran for cover.

When the speedometer reached 50, the extreme peak of low gear, he stabbed the **D2** button, producing an eek of rubber and a momentary relaxation of the engine's wild moan. The needle wobbled past 85 and he turned up the radio to max, screaming along with Ian Anderson:

> *Do you still remember*
> *December's foggy freeze*

*When the ice that*
*Clings on to your beard is*
*Screaming agony*

Consumed by the ruthless passion of the music, he passed a slow mover at over ninety, his hand flashing high in a virtuoso flourish. He sucked a few more ounces from a quart of Gallo Tokay, then jammed the bottle back between his thighs, whence it poked out like, yes, some phallic yawp.

The car's lights and noise diminished and evaporated. In a moment, with a croak and a chirp, the nighttime rejoined its rightful thrum.

—◊◊◊—

And now this night, pitched toward the dawn, Booth writhing with a fitful, inflamed joy in the squalid nether hours of a Louisiana honky tonk. The Delta Club, a bucket of blood on the outskirts of town, drinking Jax beer with the recently dead or the soon to be. A doomed soiree, during which he came to the truth that Gary was the victim of a peculiar personality disorder. Booth shared this wisdom with the others, bellowing with beer and dancing cheek to cheek with a crazed, clutching woman he believed to be the former wife of a former friend.

Also, at some point, with someone, there was a conversation about music, the day in 1966 when Dick Clark's Cavalcade of Stars came to town. Booth felt it was important to emphasize that he had actually *been there*, that afternoon when he and Gary and Eric and Wylie had used fake press passes to attend the press conference at the Holiday Inn where the Yardbirds, in high British cotton, had held forth in a slightly condescending way.

A question had been asked, seriously, by one of the reporters, regarding the absence of Jeff Beck. Keith Relf had answered that he, referring to Beck, had "a bone in his leg." It was an old joke, even then, but it drew raucous laughter from Jimmy Page and the others. Booth pointed out that this was a historical fact and could be checked out, if necessary.

Still later, an acrid steam rising from the gravel into the boneshaking clarity of headlights at 4 o'clock in the morning. And Booth's wan face comes up between his trembling hands over the tan hood of a Chrysler, vomit-flecked drool streaming from his chin.

A voice said: "Hey, get the fuck away from my car, sport." Someone pulled at his arm. Booth looked up into a face and wiped his lips with his sleeve. His mouth opened.

"...don't tell me shit about playing guitar, baby. I was there the night when Jeff Beck quit the Yardbirds."

"Yardbirds, my ass. Hippie bunch of faggots, anyway." Rough laughter shared at Booth's expense, then the impact of something squarely against the forehead.

Booth felt the fingers of his right hand being licked and sucked. It caused him to suffer an erection, which he tried to press into submission. Squirming slowly awake, a harrowing dream dissolving to the reality of hangover in the front seat of his Rambler.

He squinted cautiously over his shoulder, down his right arm, dangling outside the open front door, to find a creature hunched up and nuzzling intently at the hand. Rat's eye and unspeakable lips drawn back from needle teeth, thin matted fur, a gray tongue licking in the cold light of dawn. Booth yanked away in horror, racking his hand violently against the roof.

*"Motherfucker!"* A useless, tangled kick at the thing, screaming feebly, *"You sonofabitch! Get away from me!"* Dragging his arm inside to examine the hand, injured and clotted. He cast a horrified look out the window, hoping for a delusion, instead sees the scaly tail disappear under the car. The tip touched the dust twice, making a little exclamation point. Devil tooth in my flesh for sure. Well, at least I can see I have pants on and that's a hopeful sign. Fading back into irresistible sleep.

Waking later to the grind and clank of machinery. Booth got out of the passenger seat with upturned palms and a face of good-natured surprise worn for the bulldozer driver. A quick friendly wave to show that everything was just fine, then into the driver's seat, his right hand throbbing and powerless on the steering wheel.

Where have I landed myself now? Something of Hieronymus Bosch here. No, sanitary landfill, with a smell like crushed sage and the scavenging by squawking gulls and the poor. Both of the above looked at Booth with frank disapproval as he drove by, waving inoffensively. I hope it's not a workday or one of expectation. Once out of sight, he stopped and twisted the mirror around to see his face.

Oh, I wonder if I could become a spirit and be lifted away? Hair pushed up in front and a knot on the forehead. Bit of vomit on the clothes and, yes, a lagoon of it on the floorboard. And there was an animal involved here somehow, a possum I believe. These derelict terrors multiplying in my swollen, angelic face.

—◆—

Take this road here, then. Down onto the levee, under the bridge and out of sight. Take a few minutes to let the head clear. Just sort of get a grip on things...

*Suddenly, like the flash of a hatchet strike, came the undeniable vision of Gary's flat white face saying those cold and terminal words.*

Oh, my life just went over a cliff. There's not much hope it survived. Not after a fall like that. Hundreds of feet to the rocks. Well, it was such a silly thing, anyway. But brave, though, in the face of all that hatred and accusation. And in the pale light of this ordinary morning, parked beneath the very bridge supporting the road which led to Reno, his shoulders hunched and knees squeezed together, Booth cast down his eyes and wept.

The car was tilted toward the mud and the garfish of the Red River. Something rolls out from under the seat and bumps the heel of Booth's right foot. He looks down and discovers a forgotten bottle of Annie Green Springs, almost half-full.

—◆—

Is that the angels singing? No, lamentations, I believe. A chorus of it, swelling out onto this bleak, sun-laced street. Booth discovers himself lying vagrant, this time in freshly mown grass.

He looks around carefully. Exposed. Not naked, God be thanked, but in the broadest of daylight, outdoors for all to see. Oh, raise the boom, and please don't let Jesus find me right now. Hush these bleating terrors and pluck these cosmic thorns gently from my brow.

A medieval passion play. That's where I am. All the king's men watching, on their pounding, steaming steeds. Hear the leather grunt of a skewered Amazon toad as it roasts over a smoky fire, dripping its juice in lethal sizzles. Just a little musing to balance my thoughts at this precious moment.

Well, depending on the day, and the time, I'll just call in sick. Of course, if it's too late for sick call, as I suspect from experience that it is, just stick out my thumb in a westerly direction. Or some other pink and wiggling appendage. Go to Flagstaff and become a commissioner. Dress up like a Fabulous Furry Freak Brother and attend all the town meetings, with my pet possum on a string.

Why would I think these distressing thoughts on such a fair day? The sky is blue. *Le ciel est bleu.* Blew. Blooey. Blown, as in my chances, or at least my cover.

And where is my car? I was distinctly in it last night. I remember it clearly, provided that was the night in question.

A green four-door Galaxie passes by, with tires bumping on the disintegrating concrete. Children looking at me from the back window, their eyes wide and telling Daddy. One of these days I'll catch the little fuckers in an unfortunate situation and turn these ghastly, splattered tables on them.

Booth rises from the ground, a swarm of paramecia swimming in front of his eyes. Brushing off debris and looking around anxiously for further passersby. No problem here. Just a little privacy is all I ask, to hide my nether self. A bit of vomit there. If properly analyzed, we could determine the ingredients of my last supper, and the time it was expelled. Just enter all the terms into the right equation, properly normalized for things like the relative humidity, phase of the moon, and the shifting mood of God. Basic forensics.

Taking a few readings, Booth determines he is in Bringhurst Park. With a little further reckoning, he realizes that Skippy's, on the far edge of the park, was his most likely point of departure, and a good chance that his car is there.

Well, a walk will do me good, as long as it doesn't kill me. Far too much decadence here anyway, particularly amongst the young. I'll set a positive example. He steps out quickly, swinging the arms. Off to his left, a hundred yards or so by abstract reckoning, he hears the screech of a monkey from the decrepit little zoo. A chicken, a fox, and an amorous simian of some description.

Sure enough, his Rambler is waiting in Skippy's parking lot, and for a change, all the tires are round. Astoundingly, the Les Paul and the Twin Reverb are still sitting on the back seat.

Booth huffs across Masonic drive, waves of debauchery rising off him into the sopping Sabbath air, naked to these air-conditioned carloads of Baptists, Methodists and lesser parishioners in their church clothes. Where can I get a beer? Skippy's closed until 3. What time is it now? He squints at the blinding sun, learns nothing except that his mother was right. Don't look at the sun. Gets blindly into the Rambler, finds the key already in the slot. Have to be more careful about that. Some child could come by, peek in, take a joy ride to an unfortunate end. Booth twists the key, feels a lump in the grind of starter. Try it again. This time, the last possible electron bumbling through the rotten cables, the engine flumped into shaking, smoky life.

Booth sticks out his blasphemous sweating head, with squinted eyes and furrowed brow, into the dripping sunshine of Sunday at noon, executes a strictly legal three-point turn-around, then bumps carefully onto the broken escarpments of Masonic Drive.

*See him make it*
*Up the street*
*Ricket legs*
*And hobbled feet*

*Him mumbo something*
*Him jumbo back*
*R X R*
*with clacking track*

*See him hunch*
*Past weeds and such*
*Long on empty*
*Short on luck*

—⚋—

And now, no comfort.

No fame and no light and especially no money.

Waking up here at some vague time, covered with random clothing in this freezing room. Mother outside the door, tapping gently. Likely with her hand out for money and that is the pose assumed by most of those I know right now. Only piddling amounts of change owing, anyway, the way I look at it. Sell off a bit of stock and square all my debts. Worldly belongings only weigh a man down in his quest for the inferno or that grail thing. A sacred scrap of pewter, slick with blood and loathing.

He heaved himself to a sitting position with shoulders sloped. There was another knock at the door.

"Mom, I don't think I can handle anything right now, if you don't mind. I..."

"Mr. Malone's here."

Oh no. Another innocent, hateful intrusion, tightening the killing ring. Neanderthals falling upon a baby mammoth, bleeding and weakened by their spearings. See me in the middle, trumpeting my final screams in the nightmare snow.

"Hang on a minute." He pulled on a stiffened pair of double knit bellbottoms and a cotton tee shirt. A shank of pain shot up his right arm. Booth raises his hand up to see. He carefully bent each finger in turn to check for fractures. Opened the door and down the hall to the living room, which was laden with a feeling of having been discussed.

Malone sitting there on the sofa there with a leg crossed. Starched shirt and collar buttoned. His cigarette smoke hung in the stagnant air, incandescent in the evening sun.

"Hi, Wes. I just came by to pick up the key to the warehouse. Hope this isn't a bad time." Standing up, prepared to terminate this affair in the least offensive way.

"Mr. Malone, do you think we could talk outside for a minute?" His look of mild surprise, a glance at my mother.

"Well sure."

Outside on the front steps, that certain mood of evening in the tapering tail of a hangover. A world made of melancholy and cloth, enveloped by the sick scent of these stinking bushes next to the porch, brooding under the fatal sky.

"Mr. Malone, I wonder if you've already filled this position? I know it's a little late, and I know I kind of screwed things up, but..." Casting the eyes downward.

"How do you mean?" Bending his neck to search Booth's face.

"I'm going to be needing a job. To help my mother out."

"Really." He paused. "What became of your band idea?"

"Well, you know, it was a strange thing. Almost tragic. Just before things really got rolling the main guy and a couple of others were forced off the road by another car. Flipped. The police think it was a drunk. Anyway, they were lucky they weren't all killed. As it was, a lot of the equipment was destroyed and there's still a chance the leader may lose his nose."

"Good God. I'm really sorry to hear that." A long pause, jangling the change in his pocket, face creased in thought. "Well, hmmm..." Malone looked across the yard. He took a tiny black note book out of his shirt pocket. Clicking a ball point pen with his thumb. Rapidly.

"I'd like to see you get this job, Wes, but to be real honest I've got to know I can count on you. It's real important to be reliable in this business. This band thing..."

"Oh I can understand. And I'm sure I'd be having the same thoughts you are. The doubts and such. I can only say that I'm sorry for the inconvenience and that I'll really put my best foot forward here."

"I'll tell you what. I know you and your mama are in a fix and I'd like to help out. Let me make a couple of phone calls and I'll get back to you later this evening. How about that?" His eyes squinting inquisitively. "What happened to your head? And your hand looks kinda swole up."

Booth glances at his car, the driver's door standing open. "Oh...that dratted car. Opened the door a little enthusiastically and it kicked back on me." Booth held out his left hand for the shake.

"I really appreciate this, Mr. Malone. And I know my mother will be relieved, too." Snapping the fingers in afterthought now, punctuating this atmosphere of forthrightness. "Oh, let me run get that key for you."

"Why don't you just hang on to it for right now. I'll be back by here later if I need to pick it up."

—⁓—

And on Tuesday, in Zwolle, Booth ran afoul of a company rule. Malone points it out:

"One thing to be real careful of is when you write up the order. See this column here?"

On Wednesday, Booth discovers he is in violation of an unwritten company rule. "I remember you saying there was no dress code, Mr. Malone."

"Well, no, but I figger it's jest plain common sense to wear socks, Wes."

On Thursday, in Colfax, just as Booth enters the town, a bum rushed across the street. He accosted a woman on the opposite side. The woman shrank away from his ragged bobbing head. Booth rolls down the window of the van and hears the word "Pharisee." A preachment here in this quaint country town.

Looking into the future, I can see myself driving this same van one day very soon. My clipboard, my pricing gun with its stickers, that feather abomination back there, poking out of a crate like a Pawnee scalp on a stick. But now I'm thirty-four, and have married the woman of every man's dream. And she has popped out a few Boothlings, squalling up in harmony for Daddy. Dinner with the in-laws on Sundays, and they think I'm just the best thing ever. Upstanding. Forthright. Solid.

That's me, alright.

Please pass the grits.

—◆◆◆—

A Friday, and find Booth socializing with Eric in the Happy Hollow. "Those were the days, weren't they, Eric?"

Days of wine and rosy young girls and the violence of our drums and guitars. Those high speed runs on stolen booze and stupidity and luck that was thinner than air. All the tender young daughters of prominent people here in this town. In fact, Eric, although I've never mentioned this, there was your own sister, fat and sweet on the front seat of your very '53 Plymouth. Right in front of your father's house and that was one night I sweated for quite a while, the stark possibility of a fat baby Booth and you for a brother-in-law. Is she still fat? No longer sweet on me, I trust. It's a terror the things a man will remember some mornings after a social evening of cheap sweet wine.

A tall, stained ceiling here, with slowly turning fans and hanging tubes of light. Squeak of cubed chalk and the angles formed by elbows and pool sticks. The triangular rack of round balls. Lot of geometry here. Booth lights up a Winston, sucking the smoke into his ribcage covered with an Army fatigue shirt, Spec 4 insignia on the shoulders above hacked-off sleeves.

Lightning flared outside. Booth tipped up his mug of beer, eyes sliding nervously sideways. But safe here amongst these people and this beer. And that whiskey, too, if necessary.

"Well, what's the word, Eric? Any strange honey on your stinger?"

"Same old honey...Hey, that was a fucked up deal with Gary, man. But I kinda warned you he was gonna be a hard-ass."

"Ah, water under the bridge, Eric. Spilled milk, you dig?"

Eric looks at him for a minute. "So, how's the route thing going?"

Booth has been drinking for an hour. "Oh, great. Actually, it's very fulfilling in a lot of unexpected ways. Just this morning I was able to help a poor old man out. Corn plasters. And a couple of days ago there was the woman looking for a remedy for her genital warts..."

A burst of rude laughter down the bar and the predatory stares of three leering, vandal faces. Rudy and the Dubrocs. Looking at me in the most uncivil fashion. Eric says, "Shit. I should have known those assholes were going to take up residence here after they got kicked out of the Flame."

Now a remark from the largest Dubroc.

"Hey Booth."

Ignore him, never spoke to me before. But I feel a vague history resolving into focus here.

"Hey, guitar picker, I'm talking to you. With the army uniform. Looks like it'd be kinda tough playin' guitar with those knuckles banged up like that. How'd that happen, anyway?" Rudy snickers.

Booth draining his beer, considering this a rock or a hard place.

"Man, fuck this guy, Booth." Eric letting his beer do my talking for me. Best to make some response, though. Otherwise be deemed a coward, die a thousand tiny deaths. Booth turns with unwilling resolve in the arena of anticipation and snickers. Picks up his crutches and humps toward the Dubrocs. At a distance of five feet, he brought the right crutch up and aimed the rubber end at the Dubroc's pocked face. "Some reason you're demeaning me, sir?"

Without preamble, the thug grabbed the crutch end and twisted. A whim of chance lodged the rubber armpit cradle in the right pocket of Booth's shirt. Seeing the dice of fate tumble uncharacteristically in his favor, the lunk quickly rotated the crutch, tangling the shirt until it balled up, turning Booth and forcing him up against the bar like a dog on the end of a noose-stick, his right arm trapped in the fabric. From this ridiculous position, Booth flailed the air behind him absurdly with his left crutch. The Dubroc grabbed this unavailing weapon, and with Booth's forearm entangled in the bouts of the thing, now had him like a burro between its traces.

Through the hedge of whiskey bottles and gin, Booth can see his anguished face in the mirror, mouth open and grunting helplessly. He can also see his captor, a foul smirk on his triumphant, stupid face. The smaller Dubroc reached forward and flipped Booth's Indian headband up so that it sat on his head like an ass-backward tiara.

Then another face appears in the mirror, barely within Booth's sight. Short hair, drooping mustache, and eyes like Rasputin. The man says, reasonably, "Now, I'm thinking maybe you ought to have a little more respect for a veteran. Why not drop those things and let's all be friends here."

Booth can feel his restraints loosen slightly.

The Dubroc says, "This fish here? You want me to throw him back? I had a little talk with him the other night out at the Delta. Thinks he's some kind of big time guitar player. In fact, I'm a little surprised to see him after the talk we had. I flat told him I didn't want to see his hippie ass around." Addresses Booth. "You remembering that now, Tonto?" Shoves Booth into the bar again as an exclamation point, then drops the crutches.

Again lightning and now drops of rain, a rippling thump of thunder. Booth turns around, rearranges his vestment. Reaches for a heavy amber ashtray on the bar, but holds his fire. The stranger stands opposite the Dubroc with legs spread, arms crossed, his left hand at the right elbow, gripping the handle of a mug of beer. Brow ridge like a Neanderthal.

The big Dubroc speaks to the interloper. "You Tonto's podner, podner?" Rudy and the shorter Dubroc assume flanking stances. "You the Lone Ranger?" This last tickled Rudy and the smaller one into snuffling giggles. Booth consolidates his grip on the ashtray.

The short-haired man considered this quip reasonably, head nodding in appreciation. The rain outside came down in a gray deluge. "You know, that's a funny joke. You must have experience making jokes." He paused, looking right and left at the other two, then was seen to lean forward and whisper something to the big one. He straightened back up.

There was a moment of dawning on the man's face, the grin flashing to a stupid rage, then he made his move. Instantly, he received the thick octagonal bottom of a backhand beer mug across his cheekbone and nose bridge. An orb of beer wobbled airborne and golden in the mug's wake, the man's shirt bulging like a sail.

*"Goddamn it!"* the cracker sputtered, staggering sideways in shock, hand up to catch the blood and teeth. *"Fuck, man, shit!"* Eyes wide open at the quantity of blood and snot strung between his fingers. Before the beer hit the floor, the man on

his right went double from a foot lashed under his ribs, his breath gone in a ragged screech. The uninvolved scattered away in an upturning of chairs. The man dropped the beer mug and grabbed Rudy's head by its ears. Over the sounds of moans and gagging he spat an obscene scenario into the face, wolfman eyes daring any muscle to move.

"Now what you figure, redneck? Am I the Lone Ranger? Maybe I'm a faggot, too. How 'bout you and me in the back room and we'll find out, huh?" He paused, then stood back, face clotted with fury. Rudy stood in a cower, stock still, waiting for his fate.

Booth backed up against the bar, watching with a thought of holy fuck, who is that, Eric? Both of them waiting for the next move, wondering at the boundaries of this violence.

The man propelled Rudy, using an ear as a handle, after his confederates, helping each other hump away from their disgrace, wheezing, bleeding and threatening. Everybody smirking at the exit of the losers. Once outside the door, the one with the broken face was heard to say, defiantly slobbering blood into the rain, "...ain't no way, Bubba. *Nunh unh!* Get my fuckin' equalizer outta the truck!" But he allowed himself to be restrained by the others.

Rudy, the only one unmaimed, said, "Fuck that shit, Henry. I think we just got our ass equalized."

Inside, chairs being picked up, the exclamations and laughter of relief and the roughly veiled fawning of warrior worship.

Now the fighter picks up the beer mug and walks up to Booth with his hand extended. Says this:

"Name's Andries. Cole Andries, and man, I hate a fucking redneck." He set the mug on the bar, its bottom pasted with gore and a small swatch of mustache. "Don't you? I gotta watch it though. Sometimes I get out of hand." He accepted a beer from Eric.

"Well anyone could. I've done it myself," said Booth, looking warily at the beer mug. He introduced himself and Eric. Andries fixed Booth with a look.

"You ok, man?"

"Yeah, no problem. Thanks for the help."

"Did I hear you boys say something about playing in a band?"

Booth glanced at Eric. "Well, we used to. A couple of years back."

"I thought so. I heard you talking and put two and two together." He lit a cigarette. "You know Jill Betts?"

Booth's instant recollection of a situation one night after a gig, his fingers just under the hem of Jill's shorts, a palpitating memory of her responding moan just before interruption by the outbreak of a brawl outside the band's van.

Warily, "Yeah, right, from school. Out at LSUA." Looking at Andries' eyes for signs of murder.

Eric's bright chirp. "You know Jill too? We went to Bolton together, man."

"Well it's a small world, ain't it? I hooked up with her out in California. Berkeley..."

Eric, enthusiastically, "No shit? Yeah, Booth, remember she said she was going out there..." Booth clearing his throat, trying to create a force field to shut Eric up before he remembered anything fatal.

"Seems like, yeah..."

But Andries' face free of intent. "Anyway, she talks a lot about the band you guys had. What was the name again?"

"The Remains."

"Yep, that's the one." Andries held up his mug. "Here's to the band, then. Why don't we move over to this table. Give us some room to spread out."

Drinking late into the night, cocooned from the dying storm, rain pellets bright in the headlights of cars scarfing water blackly over the curb out front. Talking about concerts and trips of acid and cars and hitchhiking girls, of colleges attended and colleges dropped out of or expelled from. Dope smoked and music played and machine guns fired and revels performed in New York and New Jersey and Texas.

At one point, Booth returns from the john and leans his crutches against the shuffleboard table. Andries looks at Booth. "Where were you when you got hit, man?

"Ah, up close to Plei Ku. Just a touch of shrapnel."

"Tough, man. The docs figure it'll get better?"

"They don't really seem to know. It's kind of off and on—a nerve thing."

At the end, lights on, last call, Andries said, "Hey, dig it, the old lady and me are having a party tomorrow night. I think you guys oughta bring your shit out and jam. There's another coupla guys, some connection with some friend of Jill's, I forget what. But they're comin up from New Orleans and bringing some guitars and some kinda P.A. system. You gonna be able to play with that hand?"

Eric holding up his mug for the last of the beer. "Hey, man, Booth could get his hand cut off and play with the nub, if you give him enough beer. Right, Booth?"

"I'm sure you've got me mixed up with someone else, Eric..."

"Oh, we got some beer comin'. About four kegs, last I heard."

"Well, I'll do the best I can, then. Think Cheryl'll let you go, Eric?"

"Fuck that," said Andries. "Bring your old lady with you. She'll dig it."

Booth and Eric start out. As they reach the door, there is a touch on Booth's shoulder, and he turns to see. Andries is standing there, holding out Booth's crutches.

"Here you go, man." A brief, neutral look, then "See you tomorrow night. Four miles up the old Boyce Road, big white house on the left. Look for all the cars."

## five

# *lenna*

Booth turned the Rambler off the wet levee road west of town, his arm out to stabilize the amplifier on the front seat.

Twenty cars under the oaks, lining both sides of the long gravel driveway. Booth's car rocked sideways through last night's rain puddles, small waves washing through the grass. A forlorn flash of estuary hissing through his mind.

Cheryl from the back seat, "Do you know any of these people, Wesley?"

"Just that guy Andries. Eric knows him as well as I do. I'd have to caution against starting an altercation with him, though."

Two barbecue pits smoking under the carport. Three Harley Davidsons, ominously heeled over on their side stands, chopped to the bone and glitter bright, bedrolls lashed to the forks. The challenging stares of three ruffians as Booth eased the car carefully into the carport to unload the equipment.

Eric's blond head turning nervously in the mirror. "I hope you got the right place here, Booth. We're liable to wind up over that fire."

But now Andries stepping out the screen door, arm around Jill, her brown curls cascading from beneath a blue bandana, flashing eyes, lumberjack shirt tied at the waist and blue jean cutoffs. Standing three steps up from the gravel as Booth got out of the car. Two hounds wagging happily around his legs.

"All right, all right, the band's here. You have any trouble finding the place?"

"Nope, just followed the directions and here we are. Should we get this stuff out now or what?"

An ear-splitting screech and heads ducking for cover. Then an amplified voice inside the house. "Whoa, *get* back. Test one two three test. Testing one two..." Applause.

Andries' face grinning. "Sounds like Tuck's got us up and running. Let's bring your shit in." He set his beer down on the balustrade. "You boys know Jill, right? She's my old lady. Just like old home week, huh, babe?" Those eyes, but mine straight ahead and innocent of lusting, in the interest of my life.

"Wesley, how *are* you?" That same evocative smile, her arms up for an embrace. "How long has it been, now?" Her hand reaching out to squeeze Eric's arm.

"Seems like a few moons. Eric and I were just talking about it."

"Oh, hey. This is my wife. Cheryl." Eric brings her up next to him, a wide-eyed look on her face.

"Yeah, Jill, remember that time we all went up to Red Dirt? I was thinking maybe you and Cheryl met around then." Eric was on safe ground, having been coached away from any inflammatory recollections.

Into the house now, both crutches under the right armpit, guitar case in the left hand. Andries easily one-handing the eighty pound amplifier. Hardwood floor and the smell of food and marijuana. People in a throng, beer cans and Dixie cups, a Stratocaster strapped diagonally across a Marshall half stack, the pilot light glowing redly.

Booth's eyes swiveling slowly around this room with people milling. A beer in his hand now and a joint offered, pinched in an alligator clip. Swilling the beer, winking at Eric, his arms full of drum hardware. Now someone picking up the Strat, thin hair reaching his beltline, hand up for the brotherhood clasp.

"All right, man, you must be the dudes Andries hooked up with. My name's Tuck, man, and I'm some kinda fucked up." Looking at the equipment. "Hey, all right, a Twin. And a Les Paul, right?"

Booth draining a Dixie cup of beer. Hanging on his crutches outside with Eric and Cheryl in the midst of feeding, sausages and chicken and meat, red with sauces. Wild laughter and Jethro Tull on the stereo, wired through the P.A. speakers.

> *Our father high in heaven, smile down upon your son*
> *Who's busy with his money games, his women and his gun*
> *Oh Jesus save me*

Two of the three bikers were flipping knives into the air and catching them, the object apparently to do so without significant bloodletting.

See Jill standing away from the action, toking on a joint, her jaw thrust forward to avoid spark holes in the shirt. Handing the clip to a girl with short dark hair. Halter top and hip huggers, bells over sandals, a certain demeanor about her. Booth looking to catch her eye.

Suddenly his neck was grabbed from behind and Andries' voice saying roughly, "Well how about it, Booth? You havin' a good time?" Looking into Booth's cup. "You need some more beer, man." He turned slightly and plucked a quart of beer from the loose grip of one of the bikers.

"What the fuck...?" Turning with an incredulous look, beard and bandana, the forehead wrinkled. An instinctive shrinking away.

Andries pouring the beer into Booth's cup. "Pardon? Oh, hey, Bone. You don't mind if my man here has a sip, do you? He ran a little dry." Andries' look of mild amusement, eyes like pistol bores. "Booth here's the guitar player. Can't let the band get thirsty, right? You met Redbone yet, Booth?" He handed the empty back to the biker and turned away, winking at Booth. "How's that, now? A little better, huh?"

See Cheryl's pale face, Eric's eyes rolling away from the gaze of the biker, riveted on Andries' shoulders. Booth's muscles tensing for flight. But in a moment, Redbone turned sullenly and walked over to the row of kegs, bending over to fill the quart back up.

"You know that guy pretty well? He and his buddies look kinda, well..." See Redbone over there, his thumb hooked awkwardly in a pocket, face splotched red and white, glaring at Andries' back.

Andries snorted, a faint smile. "I don't think you need to worry about them." A fat girl with red hair tugged at the sleeve of Andries' tee shirt, a joint inverted in her mouth. He turned and sucked in the dirty yellow-gray plume of a shotgun hit.

Holding it down with squinted eyes, then "Hey, man, when you guys gonna play something?"

"Pretty quick, I guess...say, Cole, who's that girl Jill's talking to?"

"Which one?" Andries looking, now two more in the group with Jill.

"Short hair. With the bells."

"Friend of Jill's from Tulane. Or works there, something. Can't remember her name. Nice tits, though."

Booth now with the Les Paul slung over his shoulder and Eric running paradiddles from toms to the snare. Going through the tuning routine with Tuck and Tommy, the bass player. People standing around, looking at the equipment. The crystalline tone of the Strat countered by the smooth menace of the Gibson. Hear a girl ask Tommy, "Where ya'll from? It seems like I know you from somewhere."

"Which one you wanta do, man?"

"How bout Johnny B. Goode?"

"You wanta be lead or what?"

"You go ahead and start, then we can trade off. In B, right?"

"All right, everbody ready?"

Tuck launched the song with a hot intro, Tommy moving to the mike. *"Way down in Loosiana, close to Noo Awleens..."* Hear a shout as people started dancing. Even those outside moving to the sound, coming inside to see, Booth's fingers adding a fill in thirds over the familiar shuffle. Now time for the lead and Tuck giving Booth the nod.

The fluid vista of music, Booth navigating by feel and intuition, immersed in the matrix of patterns. Look up at the end of the ride to see the look of respect in the eyes of the watchers. Actual applause with whoops and hollering mixed in. And there's that same girl near the back wall, looking at me, glass of wine and her eyes looking at mine. Hold the head up and smile and I think that was a look of reception. But now a man moving up next to her, joint in his fingers, an arm casually over her shoulders.

Tommy poked Booth's shoulder with the head of his guitar to warn of the finish, and Booth wrapped it up with a stinging burst of pentatonic triplets. Hear immoderate shouting and looks of admiration on the faces of Tommy and Tuck, turn to see Eric's wink. A storm of requests now as people swarmed their corner. Booth looking over the heads to see the girl, vanished.

Jill came up with a pitcher of beer to pour into their cups while the other three decided on the next song. "God, Wesley, y'all sound great together. I'm so glad you ran into Cole. I still remember those parties we used to have out at the Station, don't you?"

Booth's head still weaving to look for the girl. "Uh, listen, I don't know if I'd mention all that old stuff to Cole. He doesn't seem like..."

"You're right. He's not. But don't worry, I won't say anything to him. Anyway, he likes you. He said so this morning. He said you seem like a pretty smart guy. He likes smart people."

"Is that right? Well...all right." Booth's guitar slung casually, the head pointed down, like an M-16. "Oh, hey...who's that girl you were talking to a while ago?"

"Which one? Hold out your cup."

"The one with the short hair. Bell bottoms. Sorta curvy."

"Oh." A look of knowing. "That's Lenna."

"Lenna?"

"Lenna Steadman. Funny you should ask. She asked me the same thing about you just a few minutes ago."

"Really? I..."

"Actually, you should talk to her. She's got some experience in the music business. Partied with some people you've heard of..."

"So how do you know her?"

"I met her at a Creedence concert out in California last year. We knew a couple of the same people, roadies and such. We stayed in touch, and when I found out she'd landed in New Orleans I told her to come up and visit. They've been here a couple of days, but they're heading back tomorrow."

Tuck's face intervening. "Hey, man, let's boogie. These people wanna hear some Hendrix. You know *Foxy Lady?*"

Booth's eyes intent on Jill. "Well, who's that dude...her boyfriend?"

"His name's Bobby something." She rolled her eyes up with those lashes. "I don't really know him. Some kind of finance guy. But to tell you the truth, it just sounds temporary to me, at least from talking to her."

Tuck again, insistently. "Hey, man...*Foxy Lady?*"

Booth drank off half the cup of beer and set it down on his amp. "You mean the one in F sharp? Sounds like this?" His pick flicked the G string like striking a match, fingers beginning that trademark trill, a wink at Jill. Turning to face the amplifier, he turned the volume up a couple of numbers. The maddened hornet whine of the Twin swelling to an engorged feedback howl, people backing away in a wave. Sustain it just a breath longer, then nod to the others, slide down to the seven plus nine power chord, see the crowd surge in league. Tommy's voice a passable imitation of Hendrix'. *"You know ...you're a cute little heartbreaker...ah, Foxy."* Hear the bass walk up under the vocal.

A little later, taking a break, Booth and the others were surrounded by excitement and talk.

"...no shit man, we got this thing going out in Metarie. Y'all gotta come down."

"Where?" Booth still standing with the Les Paul, wiping down the neck prior to laying it in the case.

"Metarie, man." Tommy's chin tucked down, eyes full of earnestness, speaking in the strained voice of one holding down a toke. "It's right outside Noo Awlens. This is for real, man. All we need is guitar and drums and we got the bookings already lined up."

"It sounds great, but I can't make it." Eric's woeful eyes, the pulse of glory fading away.

"How come, man? Too far to go?"

"Too married to go." He took a swallow of beer. "Talk to Booth, though. He doesn't have the same kind of anchors."

See this scene: Nighttime, and insects wheezing around the bare bulbs in the rafters of the carport. Sweat running down Booth's neck as he tried to edge closer to where Lenna stood with Bobby. It was ten o'clock and the others were talking and laughing or dancing to the stereo. Some had disappeared drunk and giggling into the darkness beyond the edge of light. Lenna's eyes glancing up, then away, then back with a latent smile, in the lee of Bobby's attention, which was distracted by a story told by Chain, one of the bikers.

"...it was the scariest fuckin' thing I ever saw, man. The bush like opened up and there's these three gooks standin' there with AKs and belts full of grenades draped all over 'em. You shoulda seen 'em grin when they saw my M-16 layin' over there outta my reach and blood all over my leg. I could tell right then they knew I was fucked. They just sorta relaxed, you know." The biker took a swig from a bottle of whiskey. "So then they start comin' toward me, right? Talkin' that vung-tau-ho-chi-minh-poon-tang shit and grinnin' with those pointy little teeth...and, man, I'll tell you..." The fat girl with red hair handed him a hash pipe. He took a deep, carbureted hit and passed it on, holding it down so long that nothing but air came back out. "You know what I still remember, man? It was the way they smelled. When they got close enough for me to smell 'em, that fishy, smoked garbage kinda smell, that's when I knew I was gonna die." See the crowd silently listening.

"I figured it wan't worth much, but I was at least gonna try for the gun. So I sorta shifted my weight a little without 'em noticin'. When I saw one of 'em start to pull out his machete, man, that's when I made my move. I tried to jump for the rifle, about as smooth as a broke-dick flounder, right, and wound up on my face about the same time all shit broke loose." Lenna's wide-eyed gaze, lost in the story. Andries walking away from the fringe of the crowd.

"What happened, man?"

"Well, the first thing I heard was this sort of thunk, then it was quiet for about two seconds. 'Course two seconds seems like a long time in that kinda situation. Then comes this other thunk and a scream like I never heard in my life. Now I'm lookin' up, right? Still movin' for the gun, now, but lookin' to see what the fuck, since I wan't dead like I figured I would be by then. And I mean, I couldn't believe what I was lookin' at." The crowd drawing closer. The biker pulled at the gold ring in his ear.

"One of the little gooks was face down with a Coleman hatchet stickin' outta the top of his head." A gasp from those in the circle. "Another one was flappin' what was left of his right arm, maybe just above the elbow. He was the one doin' all the hollerin'. The other hunk of his arm was on the ground right next to his rifle. Me, I get to my own gun just in time to see the last one spin around with the AK-47. And guess what he runs into? This is the shit I couldn't believe. There's the King with this machete up like he's gettin' ready to lay into a baseball on Sunday afternoon." Expressions of dread on the faces in the crowd. "Man, I couldn't hardly stand to look myself. I mean, it ain't pretty, watchin' a guy get his head lopped off, even if he deserves it. But I didn't figure on what happened next. Just about the time I figure King's gonna swing that blade, the little gook drops the rifle and falls down on his knees and just lets his arms hang down with his head bowed. The one-arm guy took off like some kinda half-ass gazelle. I finally get to my rifle and look up to see what's gonna happen. I mean, I know the King well enough to know it takes him a little while to cool off and I figured the gook was a dead man. But King was just standin' there lookin' at him. The gook was sayin' some Vietnamese shit, prayin' prob'ly, and keepin' his eyes right on the King's boots."

The biker took another hit on the pipe and washed it down with a swallow of whiskey. Booth looked around at the campfire eyes of the crowd.

"Finally, after a minute or so, King relaxes, right? He could see there wan't no fight left in the little fucker after seein' his buddies get wasted like that. Sorta gave me a warm feelin', to tell you the truth, and I started tryin' to get up...and man, right then the world came apart. One second the little gook was there on his knees then *brap*, this full-auto burst and his shit was all over the bush." A horrified sound rising from the crowd.

"Me'n King hit the dirt, man, and after a second or so, this dipshit from Chicago named Wilson steps into the clearing, and he's laughin' his ass off. He shoves a new clip into the 16 and says, 'Looks like we got a fresh crop of ears here, boys,' and snickers again. He's talking about ears cause some of the front line guys used to collect the ears from all the gooks they killed.

"Man, the King comes up off the deck like a maniac. He grabs Wilson by the throat and gets him down on the ground and he's sayin' *'It was over with, man, it was fucking over with.'* Then he whips out this switchblade he used to carry and puts the blade right up next to Wilson's neck, sayin' 'You want an ear, man? You want a fuckin' ear?'

"Now I'm startin' to freak out. I'm hollerin' at him cause I can see that look in his eye and I don't want to have to explain all this shit when we get back in the world. But just then a weird thing happens. They told me later it was because of all the blood I lost and tryin' to move around. Anyway, everthing sorta faded out on me. The next thing I know I wake up in the hospital back in Da Nang with these two guys from C.I.D. yammerin' at me about the King and this and that. And for once in my life I could tell 'em the truth with a straight face. 'I didn't see shit, I says, 'and that's the God's truth.' They didn't like that too much, but the doc told 'em it was true, that I'd been unconscious when the King drug my ass back to the dust-off.

Anyway, this guy Wilson was tryin' to press a whole buncha charges against the King and they were tryin' to get me to set things straight. They were pissed when the doc kicked 'em out." The biker leaned back against his sissy bar and unscrewed the cap of his pint of whiskey in the rising throb of silence.

A voice from the front of the listeners. "Come on, man. Don't just leave us hanging here. What happened?"

"Well, it's like I was sayin'. I just don't know. I was so fucked up on morphine I wan't even real sure what the C.I.D. dudes were talkin' about. Then we all got separated with me in the hospital and everthing and I didn't hook up with the King again 'til about six months ago. But I'm a wierd kinda guy, right? Can't leave shit lie, you know? I was through Chicago a year or so after I got out and I looked up this guy Wilson. His first name is Casimir, so it wan't really much trouble. Anyway, he meets me at this bar downtown. He comes in and he looks pretty much the same 'cept his hair is a lot longer. I can tell right off he's already been drinkin'. Pretty quick I can see it's worse than just that. We're talkin' about this and that and he starts ramblin' on about this cutoff arm and the King and all kinda shit. Then he starts actin' like he's gonna kick my ass, right? Well I'd had about all this shit I wanted and I guess the bartender did, too. He asks Wilson to leave, then he tells him to leave, then finally he shows him where the door is." Another swallow of whiskey. "I was just turnin' around to say somethin' to the barkeep when I look outside to where Wilson's tryin' to get his act together." The biker looked up. "You know they call Chicago the Windy City, right? Well, they're not just shittin', man. Just when I looked out the window this gust hit Wilson and almost knocked him over. But the thing that got me was it lifted his hair straight up."

A groan from the crowd and murmurs.

"His back was to me and I could see that both of his ears were slap gone. Yep, nothin' up underneath all that hair but two shiny pink patches of scar tissue." He looked up with a drunken smile. "And I guess that's the end of that story, huh?"

A hand on Booth's arm, making him jump. It was Jill, with a slice of cake on a paper plate.

"Pretty heavy, huh?" She looked around. "What do you think? Did I hook up with some kind of maniac?"

"Huh?"

"Cole, I mean."

"He seems OK to me, I guess. 'Course, I know three rednecks that'd give you a different story. He told you about last night, right?"

"I was asleep when he came home. He mentioned something this morning about a disagreement with some guys at the bar where y'all met. I don't ask him too many questions..." She glanced around again.

"How'd y'all meet, anyway? He doesn't seem like your kind of guy, if you know what I mean."

"It does seem weird, I bet. All those high class pre-law guys I used to date, I mean. Well, the only thing I can say is that California's a whole 'nother kind of place. Did you ever go out there?"

"Not really, just traveled through once just before the army. Seemed a little different."

"There was a whole lot of political stuff happening there when I went out in '68. I was dating a guy that was pretty heavy into that scene and that's how I met Cole. They were sort of friends."

"Cole doesn't really seem like the political type. How about we go sit down over on that swing? My back's starting to act up a little."

"I don't think he is, either. He was mostly hanging around with some motorcycle guys around then. Gypsy Jokers." The gentle rising of her breasts over the cake as they walked toward the lawn glider. "What's wrong with your back?"

"Oh, it's nothing, really. Just took a little shrapnel up near Plei Ku. So how'd y'all get together?"

Jill sopped the dew from the glider with napkins. Booth sits, shakes out a cigarette.

"Well, it was kind of strange, the circumstances, I mean. See, I was studying sociology at Berkeley then. We had to do a case study to get our master's. So this guy in my class had a party one night and Cole was there. He was hanging around with some of the bike guys, smoking dope and talking. So Thad—he was the guy in my class—and I were talking about case studies and he got this bright idea. He said he knew exactly who I ought to use."

"You're kidding. You mean Cole? I wouldn't think he'd go for something like that." Booth swallowing more beer.

"Well, you don't think I was dumb enough to tell him, do you? That's not the way you do those things. And you use an alias when you do the write-up."

"So you did it, huh? Seems a little risky."

"It was, but that's the strange thing. It's like the more I hung around him, the more natural it seemed to take risks. I mean he's a risk himself, as I'm sure you've noticed." She took a bite of the cake.

"Anyway, Thad introduced us and before long we were living together. A modern love story, huh?"

"What did he say when he found out about the case study?"

"He never did find out. And you make sure you don't say anything about it, OK? Really, I mean that, Wesley." Her eyes with that serious look. "I don't know what he'd do if he found out."

"Hey, I'm not planning on telling him anything he doesn't want to hear. I saw what happened to three guys last night that crossed him. Man, he had the whole bar paralyzed. Where'd he learn that karate stuff?"

"He was over in Vietnam, like you just heard. I'm not exactly sure what he did there, but it sounded pretty rough."

"Sure did. What do you mean, like I just heard? Are those bike guys friends of his?"

She paused, looking into his eyes. "They called Cole "The King" back in Vietnam, Wesley."

A slow dawning. "Cole's the one that guy was talking about? You're kidding. Man."

"Well, you can see where the nickname came from." That guy telling the story is named Chain. Well, really it's Mike, but the others call him Chain. He was over there with Cole. The other two are just friends of Mike's. They've been talking to Cole about some big deal in New Orleans. Pot, I expect. But I've got a feeling there's some stuff brewing between Cole and that big one."

"Redbone?" Booth looked across to where the bikers were lounging on their Harleys under the carport. "Yeah, I had that same feeling."

"Wesley, how's Howard doing?" The way these questions come up, these innocent little shocks.

He paused and blew out his cheeks. "Not too great, really, I'm afraid. He seems to be about the same as he was." He looked up. "Pretty much of a feeb, I guess."

"I'm so sorry to hear that. I still remember when y'all..."

"When we were twins? Yeah, I remember that, too. There but for the grace of that little heart murmur..."

"And your poor mom. Do the doctors know what happened?"

"Not really. They seem to think it was what happened in Camille, plus that hurricane we were in when we were kids. The one where my uncle and aunt got killed. They said sometimes this just happens...no real explanation or anything." He took a drag on his cigarette. "Hey, somebody's coming."

The figure of a girl backlit by the carport light. Booth squints up to see that it's Lenna, bending down to look in the dark.

"Jill? Here you are. Cole asked me to find you." Oh, the squirm an English accent causes. Lenna gives him a glance. "He says we need more ice."

"Lenna, I don't think you've met Wesley, have you?"

And along this road I know there is vegetation, green and pushy in the daytime, tangled and black at night. Flora–a rain forest, generally, with ghastly undergrowth of bramble flashing by unseen. Concertina wire for the innocent passerby or Boy Scout, but facilitating the passage of vermin, ticks, and reptiles wiggling.

Jill and Lenna in the front seat, Booth in the back. A half gallon Borden's milk carton is snugly between Booth's knees, washed free of dairy, tumid with his private reserve of beer from the keg. Trying to think of a way to talk to Lenna. Just the right touch of warmth and substance, show her I'm a man who cares.

*"Oh, Lenna, heh heh, do you think you'd like to join me back here where the view of this bramble is better?"*

No.

Booth flicked his cigarette out the window, eyes following the receding red arc and crash of sparks on the black road.

"So Lenna. Jill tells me you're from New Orleans."

Her head turning in the light from a passing streetlamp. "No, England, actually." Head turning back, a flag of hair tugged into the balm, leaving me here alone. But those eyes, even in the glow from the Pontiac's instrument panel.

"Uh, hm. Well hm, but I guess you're living there now, right? In New Orleans, I mean."

"For right now." She turned slightly to Jill. "Have you got a fag? I'm all out."

Booth quickly shakes one out, extending it over the seat. Her hand hesitant, then taking it. She breaks off the filter. "Thanks." Now Booth's Zippo out, hand cupped around the blue flame. See her head shake free of the smoke, her chin up innocently, but with inflammatory effect just the same.

And me here in the back seat, making small sounds.

Jill: "Lenna, did I tell you that Wesley is a writer?"

"A writer? I thought you were a musician. Weren't you playing with the band?"

Oh ho, the charade of innocence. And Jill, taking up my cause. I love the way girls conspire, when they're not laying about them with fang and claw, something I prefer to avoid.

"Well, just a bit of poetry. I kind of do both. Which do you prefer, guitarist or poet? I'm adaptable, sort of a plastic man. Like Gumby."

"Gummy?"

"Gumby. A man of unimpeachable character. Malleable, to be sure, but able to prevail in the direst of circumstance."

"I see." Lenna glances at Jill with dubious face.

Booth continues: "Weren't you standing back by the window?"

"The window?"

"The one of opportunity. Surely you noticed. There was a cool breeze coming through it. But just then I noticed a man in a suit walk up next to you, and you disappeared."

See her eyes in the yellow dimness. I perceive a slight smile, though.

Jill again: "I told you he was a writer. You can always tell by the way they talk. He's going to have a collection of his poetry published. An anthology."

"Really? Poems about Gumby?"

And in the store there was silly small talk about the selection of snacks. Booth suggests pigs' feet for the girls, cotton candy for the bikers. Booth decides that Lenna has a mouth very like Pattie Boyd. Who has, in his considered opinion, the most dangerously angelic face ever coveted by rock star or mortal man.

At one point Lenna bent over to pick up a bag of Screaming Yellow Zonkers. A birthmark was revealed beneath the right arm, spreading toward her breast like a creamy coffee spill.

Spot.

Back in the car Lenna said she wished she had bought something to drink. Booth immediately offering beer from his milk carton, overwhelming her protestations by tipping it in a fashion so her only choices were drink or be drenched. But see that look in her eyes as he controlled the flow perfectly.

Lenna wiped the froth off her upper lip with an innocent, dizzying gesture.

—◆—

Walking back in the door with Jill and Lenna, bags of ice, chips, Cool Whip, and ice cream salt. Tuck and Tommy and Eric were working through a left-handed version of *Smokestack Lightning*. Tuck motioning to come up. Feel Lenna's shoulder touch mine and I don't think that was an accident. Just have to unload these packages. Into the kitchen, broad counters crowded with plastic cups and ashtrays and purses and puddles. Put the ice down and turn to help Lenna with hers.

God damn it. Bobby right there, waiting obviously for an introduction or explanation, a mild smile under that brown mustache. The look of business about him. Double knit bell-bottoms and a sport coat. A man who knew where he was going. Muttonchops and a trace of the stare in his eyes.

"Hey, babe. We were wondering where you'd got to." His arm once again around her shoulders, but just the slightest shrinking away by Lenna, her eyes looking innocently at Booth.

"Bobby. This is Wesley. He's a good friend of Jill's. One of the musicians."

The handshake assertive, crunching with possession. "Bob Hyatt. How's it going?"

"Why, very well, sir. And yourself? How's your portfolio holding up?"

"Beg pardon?"

Booth drains the remaining half pint from his milk carton. "The girls and I were just chuckling over an article I read today about the recent fluctuation in the dollar vis-a-vis the pound. A little ripple in the old pond. Tempest in a teapot, I say. How do you see it?" See Bobby's twisted eyebrow, Lenna containing a

smile by turning her head away toward the living room. Booth
continues:

"Bit of consternation out there in the business world, I've
heard."

Now see Booth again with the Les Paul pending from his
shoulder, this time with a feeling of Lenna swelling in his chest.
And also a feeling of beer. At one point he could see Lenna
listening to the music, her eyes toward Booth while Bobby
made silent sounds at her with a face of some ire.

At ten minutes to one Booth clicks his amp to standby and
heads with intent to where Jill and Andries are standing with a
group leaving. Outside in the carport lopes the lazy idling of a
Harley. Bobby fortunately absent for the moment. Enlist Jill's aid
here in the matter of Lenna. But...

The screen door bangs suddenly open. There, with some
anonymous escort, stands Jeri, Evelyn Bachmeier's niece. Trans-
formed, to say the least, her eyes turning, fated, to lock on those of
Booth. Who was just starting to say a word to Lenna. There was a
smile frozen on Lenna's upturned face. Bobby could be seen off to
the periphery, approaching with a paper bag. The Harley pro-
duced a hissing backfire, then abruptly died.

In this silence Jeri tossed her head. "Well. Hello, Howard. I
see they've let you out again." She swayed slightly, linked her
arm with that of her companion.

"Haven't been set upon by any dogs lately, have you?"

Booth turning to explain this situation to Lenna, but Bobby
was there, filling her arms with after-party take-homes.

Booth's whispered plea. "If I could just talk to you for a minute?"

But just like that, Lenna was gone, Bobby's back a polyester rebuke. Ah, but at the edge of the pool of light from the carport, Lenna turned her head back and gave a little wave.

Lenna. Oh my.

# *hominid*

"Well, where are you off to this morning?" Mrs. Booth in her red corduroy bathrobe, making sandwiches for his lunch, as though he were a schoolboy. The white kitchen clock pointed to 6:38 on the red tickmarks. AM. *Ante meridiem*. A simple, everyday little horror.

"Uh, Jena. They're putting in a new cathouse up there and they want to have a good stock of commodities on hand."

"A *what*? Oh, I see...you're being funny again."

"Nothing funny about it, Mom. I hear the mayor and everybody is in on it. Well, you know, they have to find something for those antebellum girls to do."

She pursed her lips and shook her head, dismissively. Smoothed the hair over her ear and sat down with her cup of coffee.

Booth continues, expanding on the chatty mood. "Actually, I've been thinking about looking at some real estate while I'm up there. I understand the VA has some special programs available for snake infested seepage pits. Grants or some such."

He stands up. "Well, I better head out. The bumpkins are waiting for their ointments. Hard to mount a John Deere or greet the livestock when your hemorrhoids are sticking out like funnel shaped..." He pauses, then, "Did you know that Preparation H has come out with a new applicator tip?"

She made a face. "Is there some reason you work so hard at trying to aggravate me?"

"Oh come on, Mom. Just a little levity in the morning..."

"Levity?" Her eyes narrowed. "You think you're funny, but you seem pretty mad to me."

"Mad?"

"You act like you just hate everything. Have you looked in the mirror at the creases in your forehead?"

"I don't know how you can say that, Mom. You know very well that I'm just a little more sensitive than most of the inhabitants around here. As for the creases, it's just the natural consequence of the responsibilities I carry around like the hump on a humpback."

"Responsibilities my eye. What responsibilities?"

He looked at her and sighed. "I don't think you really understand me, mom. I frankly think I'd be a lot better off out west. Flagstaff, for example."

"Out west?" She laughed. "Don't make me laugh. That's cowboy and Indian talk. The...*inhabitants*...out there work for a living too, just like here. I don't really think it's the place for someone as"...an inflection here..."*sensitive* as you." McGee chirped brightly in agreement.

Booth squints at her, then turns to the bird, fluttering joyously around its cage. A shaft of sunshine coming through an east window lit up the little cloud of dander and guano raised by its cavorting.

Booth reaches out and shakes the cage in a friendly way, then draws a bead on the bird along a pointed finger, with squinted eye. "Hey, Mom. Any chance you know where my old air rifle wound up? That Benjamin pump Daddy bought for me when I was a kid? For some reason I've been thinking about it a lot lately."

———m———

Emerge, in the manner of an angel or a buzzard, from the unconsolidated haze of a summer morning in east-central Louisiana. Down on that road, see a white Ford Econoline van, making good time through the rising mists of midmorning and the mirrors of roadside puddles.

The driver is Wesley Booth, who is deep in mindful wanderings.

He is considering his future, in preference to the past or present, each grisly in its own way. Waft into the van itself, vicariously, and see Booth's ambitious shoulders hunched. He wears a new paisley shirt, and that pulse of Lenna ripples through his chest again. But just remain focused on the task at hand, for the moment at least.

The road makes a turn, a levee on the right, King Cotton on the left. Look out now and see these colored people with rag bandanas and wide hats working in those fatal fields, dragging long sacks filled loosely with bolls. Remember that one time as an enterprising child when I gave cotton picking a try. The husks brown and sharp, merciless on my tender schoolboy hands. Discovered it was not for me forever.

But safely here in this conditioned air, the suffering globs of Mississippi humidity squeezed out of it. In my pedestal seat, enjoying a smoke, up this gummy road to Jena, my appointment for today. Should be simple enough. Merely stock the shelves, tidy up, make a note of what needs replacing, behave nicely and then back home. Most importantly, though, pick up my first check, which is to be waiting at the store in Jena. Malone had gone to Leesville to do an initial order for a new store and, incidentally, to inspect a herd of goats he was considering as an investment. There was a level of comfort in his absence. A goatherd with a flattop.

Booth took a swig from a bottle of Royal Crown Cola. Topped it up with the bottom half of a bottle of Dr. Tichenor's antiseptic, stolen from one of the crates in back of him. For the breath, of course. The social implications. Flicks the small bottle out the window into the clutching roadside bramble. Make a note to the company about the short order.

I think there's something to this working business, in spite of my doubts. Find my rightful place in society, doing something useful at least. Red plastic crates full of cosmetics, cough medicine, wart removers, bunion treatments and tampons rattling in the back. But no hangover and that's okay with me. Thought I needed a doctor for that last one, the feel of a worm dying in the brain.

Driving into Jena, he located the I.A. Gimble Mercantile. Parked the van in an alley between the store and another brick building. Feel a slight buzz from the Tichenor's. But under admirable control, and with excellent breath. Fixing an eager smile on his face, he walks confidently into the store to greet the proprietress, a Mrs. Modine Gimble.

Booth is immediately struck by the remarkably small head on the woman. A sharp nose, the hair curled unnaturally tight. Shaking her hand, the flesh of the rural south in his palm. They exchange pleasantries. "Hasn't this weather been nice," she says. Oh, the love these people have for their weather. I could easily break her spine over my knee, or eviscerate her with this box knife. Kidding, just kidding.

"A bit humid for me, I'm afraid. I really prefer the climate in the West." Wiping a flood of sweat off his forehead.

"Well, Mr. Malone spoke well of you. He said he thought you were going to work out just fine."

"All I ask is a chance to prove myself, Mrs. Gimble. I think I can make a positive contribution." Spoken modestly, of course.

Mrs. Gimble shows Booth the health and beauty aids section, voicing a small complaint about the last man.

"He was a nice man, but he spent a little too much time talking to the girls, I thought."

"The girls?"

"Well, my nieces. They help me with inventory and stocking..." She paused. "Are you a married man, Mr. Booth?"

Oh, I get it.

"Not yet, Mrs. Gimble. But very soon. I'm engaged."

"Well, that's nice." She seemed reassured.

"Oh..." Booth makes a broad smile. "Mr. Malone said he was going to drop a check off for me..."

"Yes, I meant to mention. He called and said he left the check at our store over in Jonesville..."

"*Shit.*"

"I beg your pardon?" Her head jerks back as if slapped. "I've already sent my niece over to pick it up."

"Sorry, Mrs. Gimble." Making a grimace and reaching for his back. "Sometimes I get a sharp little twinge...a few shards of shrapnel... Um, when do you think your niece will be back?"

"Oh, I wouldn't think too long. It's not that far."

Booth surveyed the shelves. What a holy fucking dreary mess. Looks like the local urchins have been let in to squat and thrash and grunt amongst the wares, in the manner of apes. And Malone had specifically pointed out the need for tidiness and order. Only one thing to do.

"I'll just step out to the van for my things, Mrs. Gimble." He glanced at the clock. "You know, actually, I think I'd like to get a cup of coffee first. Just sit down and sort of organize my thoughts. You can see I've got my work cut out for me here. I'd like to formulate a plan of attack." A look of forthrightness. "Could I bring back a cup for you?"

"Why, yes, Mr. Booth." She looked at him for a second or two, then indicated a direction. "If you'll go up two doors this way, the Blue Spot Diner has good coffee. Just a little cream in mine, please, and thank you."

Out into the dreadful, blinding haze of August. Two doors up to the diner, Mrs. Gimble said. But the third door a bar and grill. Dub's Saloon. Booth checks his pocket. Six dollars and some change. Maybe just a grilled cheese sandwich. He pushed the door open into the cool and dark.

The lazy click, rumble and thump of pool balls. Booth up to the bar, his eyes adjusting to the darkness. A girl behind the bar, playing bar dice with a customer, bopping the cup on the hardwood. Finishing off the game with a laugh like Janis Joplin. Now with a rag, swiping the bar in front of Booth.

"What can I do you for, partner?"

"I was thinking about a grilled cheese sandwich."

"Can't do it, bud, the route man doesn't get here till around noon."

Well. Then.

"Well...how about a can of Schlitz, then."

"You got it." Short blonde hair in a boyish cut and freckles on the nose. Cut off blue jean shorts. There is the click and pssst of opening and now the cold can in front of Booth. She returns to her friend down the bar. Booth swallows a good cold slug. Nice and cool in here.

After Booth's second beer, the door flashed open, and Booth's eyes squinting from the screaming outside light. Two long-hairs come in, exchanging words of familiarity with those at the bar. They ordered beer, then into the corner where drums were set up. Booth twisting around on his barstool, lighting up a cigarette. The unsnapping of a guitar case and the blue pilot light on a rolled and pleated Kustom amplifier. There was a percussive *whump* then a potent, ethereal hiss. A quick harmonic check of the tuning. A paradiddle on the snare and SH-boom from the high hat to the bass. The drummer folded his sticks and looked to the guitarist for guidance.

"One, two, three, four," then the unmistakable double thump gateway to the lead riff of "*Whole Lotta Love*" by Led Zeppelin. Right here in downtown Jena.

But two bars out of the lead, the guitarist halted it.

"Sounds like shit without the bass line."

Booth buys three beers, sidles up to the bandstand to offer his services, pointing at the bass guitar case standing in the back.

Moments later, a Fender Precision Bass hanging around his neck, turning on the Bassman amp, he cautioned, "I can only play a couple. I've got work to do." He asked for another beer, since they were having one.

Then they ripped into it, Booth struggling with the thick bass strings, like guy wires compared to those on the Gibson. But adequately. And moving with the music and beer. A few more people coming in. A new song now. Booth following, heard it once on the radio. People paying attention. Booth raises a hand and the bar girl brings more beer.

At some point the tiny head of Mrs. Gimble was seen to appear at the small rhomboid window in the front door, peering about like a praying mantis. She seemed agitated, but didn't open the door.

Oops, I'd better get back over there. Boys, I've got to go. I've got business to attend to. There are health and beauty aids with my name written all over them. He drained his beer and shook their hands, saying he'd be back to check them out later.

And out the door. My God. I don't believe this mortal, dripping heat. I could die here, right on the street. Steps into the Blue Spot Diner and buys two Styrofoam cups of coffee, one with cream. Details make all the difference when it comes to credibility. Quickly around the side to where the truck is parked. A stack of the red plastic baskets rattling on his hand truck, he whisks business-like in the side door. Right into…

"Ah, Mrs. Gimble." Holding the cups up so as not to spill. "I'm really sorry for this delay. You won't believe this, but I ran into a man I was in the army with. We fought together in Vietnam." He hands her the cup marked cream on the lid.

Her posture was damning, and her eyes disbelieving, despite the coffee. She needs to be more trusting, I think. I'm sure she's a decent, church-going woman. I can tell by the shape of her head.

Holy Christ, what's this behind her? Long copper ringlets over eyes of glassine green. And pale shoulders that I really must touch. Without the usual penalties.

"And would this be one of your nieces?" Cleverly controlling the gusts of beer on his breath so she wouldn't know.

An uncomfortable pause, her eyes reluctant to stop pecking at mine. Finally, "Yes." Then to the girl, "Jenny, this is Mr. Booth. He's going to be very busy so please try not to disturb him."

"Just call me Wesley, Jenny." She glanced at him with a smile then looked at the floor, holding out an envelope with his name on it. Booth reaches carefully past Mrs. Gimble and takes it from the girl.

I do love the shy ones. They thrill me like no other. Nineteen, maybe twenty, and now, watching her walk away, I can't avoid the compelling image of a copper tufted mound, the delicate flower offered up in trembling surrender...

*"Mr. Booth!"*

*Yes, Jesus,* don't scare me like that. I thought a bomb had gone off.

"Could you say when you'll be through?"

Well, I'd say we're pretty much running against the tide here, Mrs. Gimble. But...

"I expect an hour or so. I'll just bring in the rest of the merchandise."

Back into the van. A drop of sweat plips onto the brown vinyl of the seat, commingling with a little dust. Unbelievable heat in here. I've heard of dogs and even children dying inside cars left in the sun like this. Wipes a gout of sweat off his forehead. I can't take this physically. Or emotionally either. I feel that my stock has slipped a notch with Mrs. Gimble. She sees me in an unfavorable light now with this delay. I really must have another beer. But cleverly.

Circling around back of the store, in uncharted chaos, sweat flowing freely under Booth's shirt. Looking for a landmark. Somewhere in this fly-humming oblivion of flattened boxes and stink of garbage under the sun. The exhaust of a central air conditioner blowing out a death of hot air. Where am I? Man found wandering, lost in plain sight.

Ah-hah. He spied a U-Tote-Em down an alley in the other direction. And another direction is a good way to go right now.

Through the heavy glass doors and to the cooler, fingers grabbing two six-packs of Schlitz. Up to the counter, two men watching my eyes.

"That'll be three seventy-four, sir."

Booth pulls the envelope out of his shirt pocket, tears off the end and extracts the pale yellow check. Delicately removes the stub. "And will you gentlemen kindly honor a check from my employer?"

One of the men takes the check and looks at it. "Sorry sir, we can only take local checks." Hands it back.

"Well, to be sure. But this isn't from some common suspect—it's from a *distributor*. Of health and beauty aids." Here Booth makes a reassuring face. "Respected company."

"Yes, but it's from Arkansas, sir. I'm afraid we'll have to ask for cash, if you don't mind."

"God damn it." Only two dollars left. Searching for change. Another sixty-one cents. He smacked it on the counter.

"Will that be enough?" Sweat in his ears.

"Two sixty—one. That'll be enough for...um...eight cans, sir."

"Well, shit, then." He rips two cans out of their rings, stacks them on top of the permissible six pack. Clumps the denied four dramatically to one side, eyes spitting hatred. "Now is it right? The calculus, I mean?"

The man plunked the beer into a bag. "Yes sir, and..." He slid a dime and a penny back across the counter "...here's your change."

"What am I supposed to do with eleven cents? Buy *real estate?*" He jammed the coins errantly into the cardboard slots on the Jerry's Kids display, rendering it askew.

Walking indignantly out the door, he heard "...no need to take offense, sir. And thank you for your business."

I feel I'm being made the object of sport of here. And I don't like it a little bit.

Headlines tomorrow:

CLERKS FOUND MURDERED, EYES POKED OUT

Subhead:

MANHUNT ON FOR LARRY, MOE OR CURLY JOE

But Booth walks calmly away with his paper bag, commodities wet and gently bonking, unseen by even the sharpest eye amongst these good burghers. Right through the steaming alley, invisible.

Back at the van, Booth checked for signs of interference. Nobody around. Mrs. Gimble inside, nervous. Malone in Leesville, fucking a goat. Into the seat quickly and the engine on. Wish I'd had the good sense to back into this damned alley. Well, just follow a straight line backwards, and rapidly, in case Mrs. Gimble is peeking out through a vent or sewer grate. He spun the engine up to a rattling whine and clicked the lever into **R**.

Erupting from between the buildings, the undercarriage grinding over the sidewalk, he almost killed a schoolboy. The boy issued a squawk and gave him the finger. Booth slammed on the brakes in the middle of the street and the back doors, unlocked, flew open. A crate shot out the back, scattering Afro Sheen, Aquanet and sewing notions across the asphalt. He cranked the wheel violently to the left and crammed the gear shift into L. Inside the store window, Mrs. Gimble could be seen making an urgent telephone call. Jenny was by her side with hands up to her mouth.

I'm afraid there are some loose ends flapping here. And a man can easily get tangled up in loose ends. Booth stomped on the gas, the left tire hopping and smoking, and the remaining crates slewed sideways to jam at the door jamb. Thank goodness for that. I'd better bring some of this shit back to Malone for bargaining power. Make him believe somebody stole this fucking van. I don't think Mrs. Gimble could prove it was me at the wheel. There was a glare on the windshield. Besides, I can always bring the size of her brain case into question, if it comes down to a court room. Call in an anatomist and have him compare it with the skull of a hominid or a chimpanzee. *Jenapithecus gimblensis.*

Booth ripped open a beer and flipped on the air conditioner, aiming the vents at his face. Just south of town he stopped, pissed accurately into a ditch, and locked the back doors.

Two hours later, the van hidden behind Skippy's, find Booth inside the bar, hands drumming the table, jukebox booming, mind fevered with beer. Telling of his escape in this cinderblock box, black walls fluorescent with hippie wisdom and DayGlo pictograms.

Andries there too, with a true tale of his own, concerning an ugliness, between these songs. He had been accused of stealing almost two hundred dollars from the office at the apartment complex where he worked as the maintenance man. But he knew that it was instead the accuser himself, the owner's son, that had stolen it. Now he had actually recovered the loot, found it in the same place where the son kept his dope.

"Well, what's your problem? You've got his ass cold." Booth's left fingers manipulating the air, imitating Eric Clapton's lead on *"Strange Brew."*

"The problem here is that I kicked the shit out of him."

"How much shit did you kick out of him?"

"Enough so I'm leaving town. Tomorrow. Everything's pretty much packed. I'm staying away just in case the little shithead calls in the law."

"Where you going? Back to California?"

"New Orleans. Jill's got this assistant teaching gig down there, and I've got some things going on too." Looks at Booth with a sly smile. "Why?"

"Oh, I'm thinking about heading west, myself. Someplace that's not gurgling in sweat. But for the moment, New Orleans has crossed my mind. Lot of music happening down there."

"Well, we're thinking about going back to Berkeley, eventually. But like I said, I got some business in New Orleans right now."

Andries pours beer into Booth's mug, then into his own. Looks up with his insinuating face. "It's that broad, ain't it?"

"What?"

"Laura, something like that? That's why you want to go, right?"

"Oh, you mean Jill's friend, the English chick? Lenna, I think."

"Hey, I can dig it. Some fine piece of ass. Sure, you can head down to New Orleans with us if you want to. We'll put you up until you get situated."

"Be OK with Jill?"

"Sure. She thinks you're cool."

"And I can probably hook up with Tuck. Sounds like they got a live thing going on down there. Thanks, man, I'll do it. But I do have two problems."

"What's that?"

"Well first, my back's sorta gimped up, so I don't know how I could help with anything heavy. But how about this?" Swig of beer. "I'll bring enough food to last…oh, a month or so, and if I haven't hooked up with the music scene or else finished that anthology by then, I'll just drift. Don't like the feel of being a freeloader."

"No sweat. What's your other problem?"

"That truckload of shit out back. I'm not real sure what to do about it."

"Let's split, then. I've got an idea."

*POW!*

A magnum burst of DEP men's styling gel flashed like a handful of diamonds in the headlights of Malone's white Ford van. Booth watching the criminal destruction of Ozark hair products, followed by drunken laughter as Andries handed over the revolver.

"See what you can do with that Listerine shit, Booth." Shouting to make himself heard over the tufts of cotton wadded in their ears.

Taking aim from the two fisted G-man stance, Booth squeezed off a round, hand shaking as he pulled against the double action. Then a sharp smack to the palm, the report like a pine board struck by a hammer. A linear disturbance down-range as the 158 grain .357 hollowpoint zipped into the undergrowth beyond the line of beauty treatments.

"Nah, look here, man. Try it single action." Andries took the revolver, showing how to thumb back the hammer. "See?"

Booth tries it, luckily producing a violent golden eruption of mouthwash.

"All right!" He drained his beer, flung the can. "Watch this shit." He quickly fired the remaining three rounds, missing with the first two. But the last opened a can of hairspray in a surprising blossom of bluish flame. Booth giggled excitedly.

"Hang on a second." Andries bent into the trunk of his black '67 GTO while Booth plucked the warm, smoking empties out of the .357's cylinder, replacing them from the box on the hood. Now Andries comes up with a Colt 45 automatic in his left hand. "Come on."

They assembled two ragged pyramids with the remaining merchandise and returned to the firing line in front of the van. Andries popped a clip into the .45 with the heel of his right hand.

"Ready?" He racked back the slide.

Booth places a call from a phone booth on Bolton Avenue:

"Can I speak to Mr. Malone, please?" There was the sound of a child calling for daddy.

"Yellow."

"Mr. Malone? This is Wesley. Wesley Booth."

"*Wesley. Where in the hell are you?* Have you talked to your mother? I've got the police out looking for you. What the heck happened up there today?"

"Listen, Mr. Malone, I had some trouble today...I got robbed."

A pause. "*Robbed?*" Pause again. "Wesley, you sure you got your story straight here?"

"I'm not sure what you mean. Two guys pulled a gun on me and hijacked the van, right outside that store up in Jena. They beat me up when they found out I didn't have any money."

"*What?*" Pauses. "Are you sure about this, Wes? I mean this isn't what I heard from Mrs. Gimble at all. Frankly, she said you'd been drinking."

"Drinking?" My incredulous inflection, Andries snickering in the background. "Those guys really might have hurt me, Mr. Malone." A pause. "To tell you the truth, the guy I caught a ride back to town with said I ought to sue. The company, I mean. Now, I'd never think about doing that, but I'm really freaked after what they did to the van."

Silence on the other end. Then tensely, "What happened to the van?"

"It scared me to death, Mr. Malone. When they started shooting I almost pissed myself, to be honest."

"*Shooting?* Well for God's sake."

"I thought I was going to lose my eyes with all that glass flying around."

"You mean the headlights?"

"And the windshield, Mr. Malone. It was like a glass hand grenade. I'm still picking pieces out of my scalp."

"Well good God Almighty. Where's the van now?"

"Still out there in the woods, I guess. I got out of there the first time they turned their back. Of course by that time they were so drunk they didn't notice."

"They were drinking?"

"Oh hell yes. They must've had three cases of beer with them. I heard them say something about knocking over a U-Tote-em somewhere."

Silence for a moment.

"Do you think you'd be able to recognize them?"

"I just wish I could, Mr. Malone. But they had these masks on. Strange masks with symbols on them. Oh, and this is really something." A pause for drama. "They were smoking marijuana." Andries spewing beer and coughing so that Malone hears.

"Who's that? Where are you?" Credibility at risk.

"Oh, I meant to tell you. I'm at Baptist Hospital in the emergency room. Some guy with emphysema here in distress."

"Wesley, it sounds like we've got some real bad actors here. Have you talked to the police yet?"

"No, I wanted to call you first thing. I'm really upset by all this."

"Well, you just calm down. I'm gonna call my brother in law. He's with the sheriff's auxiliary. Do you think you can show him where the van is?"

"Look, Mr. Malone. I don't want to seem like a candy ass or anything, but I'm not going anywhere near that place. Those guys have guns." A gulp of beer. "Tell you what though. There was one lucky thing. I recognized the place where we were."

"Good man." A pause, then, "Wesley, you best be telling me the truth now. Weldon—that's my brother in law—is not somebody you want to mess with. Now, where's the van?"

"Out at Camp Livingston. You know that place everybody calls the Icehouse? Well it was right there. They were starting a bonfire with the merchandise when I snuck off. I think they were using hairspray cans for torches."

"Jesus..."

"Have you ever seen that? It's just like a flame thrower." Booth paused for a drag on his cigarette. "I'll never forget that sight, Mr. Malone. Their heads were back and they were sort of howling while these flames lit up all those big trees out there."

# *on the lam*

Sweat ran under Booth's tee shirt in the front yard with pine trees above and crisp needles underfoot. He was loading belongings into his car. The gray Rambler idled feebly, dappled in the slanting sun. A blue fog of Rambler smoke wafted softly on the ground.

Despite his precautions, he was caught by his mother just as he was carrying the last load to the car. She did some crying, too, as she packed sandwiches for his trip, woe dripping wetly on the Holsum bread and Velveeta.

"I know you're a decent boy, Wesley, but I just don't understand what happened up there in Jena. I asked Mr. Malone when he called, and he wouldn't tell me."

"It was a misunderstanding, Mom, just a big mix-up."

"Well, why don't you explain that to Mr. Malone? I know he'd listen if you just would."

I don't think so, Mom. The only thing keeping the law out of my ass right now is that he knows he can't prove that I was responsible for any of that stuff. After all, I think it's fairly clear that I have a *condition*. Not even Mrs. Gimble would argue that.

Finally, sitting on a pillow covering the wire of the driver's seat. Mother at the Rambler's window, her unavoidable weeping.

"Mom," Reassuring with chosen words. "I'll be back soon. I've just got to get out of here for a little while until Malone realizes I wasn't the one responsible. I'll give you a call in a couple of days."

*"But where are you going? I don't even know where you're going."* A desperate, rising tone, raising a concern that she might even try to detain him here in the front yard.

"I'm just going down to New Orleans. I'll be staying with some friends. I'll send you the phone number as soon as I get it." Foot fidgeting on the gas pedal.

There was a flutter off to the right, and a blue jay flew across the yard in that dipping, intermittent way. It landed on the Rambler's hood and cranked its neck around angrily, looking directly at Booth. Then it threw back its angular head and issued a cry with primal mouth stretched wide. Booth stared.

His mother again, wet and wounded eyes looking not at Booth, but into despair. Her voice piping.

*"But what about Howard, Wesley? You can't just leave him like this, can you?"*

Finally, he drove away, with the pinched image of her face and her soprano keening like a tusk in his soul.

They left at night, in the manner of carnival workers, hunched under the burden of domestic artifacts as they labored between

Andries' house and the U-Haul trailer. Fortunately, Andries said, they had dumped most of the heavy stuff when they left California.

Finally on the road, pointed south. Not my preferred direction, but a stepping stone. A fat yellow moon emerged over the black fields south of town as they left, Booth following Andries' Pontiac, which pulled the trailer.

Booth's radio was tuned to WIBR for the sound of Janis Joplin. All these idols falling like skewered angels. A bottle of sweet wine on the seat next to him, the sour feel of it in his stomach. In the back, his guitar rode transverse on the floorboards, the amplifier on the seat side by side with the Remington Rand, stuffed and cushioned by paper bags of clothing and hastily gathered debris. Far off, to the southwest, there was a faint bloom of lightning.

And driving through Cheneyville and Bunkie and past the cutoff for Mamou. A black landscape made for dreams of swamps and a smothering culture. Gumbo, *cochon de lait* and reptiles slithering. That chanky-chank cajun music emanating. And enough water in the air to stave off drought for a ream of centuries. Air conditioning the only thing keeping us alive.

Booth tips up the bottle of Boone's Farm Wild Mountain to his trembling alien lips. I'm an alien in every sense of the word. Plunked down here in the middle of the cotton bolls and the cottonmouths. Just enough time to light a candle of happiness before it's waylaid by the dread that oozes up from this glutinous delta.

And what if the worst happens and you get shoved in? The trick, when you reach bottom, is to use just one foot to push off with. You never know what's down there under the mud and slime, and you might need the other one to kick loose if you get grabbed. That's the way I see it anyway. The sooner you learn the ropes, the less chance you'll get caught in one.

The lightning blossoms closer and more frequent, and a new noise materializes under the hood of the Rambler.

Coming at last into the city of New Orleans, a town sopping with decadence and sweat. Peeling floral wall paper and little old ladies stinking of perfume and memories of lost grandeur. In their parlors with artifacts, barricaded against the menace of those uppity nigra men out in the streets, bopping to the cheap, thin tootle of Dixieland jazz, eating corn from the cob and laughing with massive white teeth. Making deals with money and dope, right here in the French Quarter, *Vieux Carré*, wrought iron windows and loud flashy whores. Families set upon by shirtless young drunks and the gutters running with piss and vomit on festering weekend nights. City of music and romance. A *beignet* for breakfast, a cockroach in your *bisque.*

A soggy thrill to it just the same. All these lights. Safety in lights. I hate it when it's dark and stormy and I'm small and there are things that might get me. Follow these lights on the back of Andries' GTO, with the Nixon-Agnew bumper sticker.

Uptown, off St. Charles, to the house rented for them by Jill's friend Della. Half of a shotgun double, named because of its linear layout, the idea being that a shotgun fired through the front door would probably take out somebody in any room.

But not me. Up late on this thunderstorm night of arrival, electricity out, candles lighting the boxes still stacked on the floor. Rain draining out of the big oaks out front. Booth hunkered in a corner under the silent air conditioner with his Les Paul. A bottle of Boone's Farm and the latent sound of a solid body electric guitar with no juice, a tinkling shadow in the darkened room. The others passing joints around, Cole and Jill, Eddie and Della.

Booth squinting in the candlelight as his fingers played. Della, not really involved in the conversation, looked up, recognizing the tune. Singing the words softly.

*"Love me two times, babe. Love me twice today."*

After a time, Booth drifts off, hearing the voices planning, talking about old shared times. Eyes closed, safe. Rousing himself to nestle the guitar neck between two boxes and drag out his mattress. Sleeping bag on top. Into it, jeans and all. I'm a baby Cro Magnon in a deerskin wrap. Safety and peace, the adults grunting around the night fire.

I hope I don't fart in the presence of these people after I fall asleep.

And in the morning, Booth wakes up to the childhood thrill of a different place, made grander by the fizzling trail of annoyances behind him.

Scrooch back under the sheet for a quick curl. Smell bacon cooking, and coffee. The sound of a toilet flushing and the bump of feet as the others come to their fearless grips with the day.

Booth sits up, and peeks out to see sunlit leaves and petals of a flower bush. I know there is a name for this particular plant, but not what it is. Then, the next-door neighbor's house, with clothes sagging on a clothesline in the back yard. And see a black-haired woman snapping a rug, then examining it closely, as if to be sure a spot of dog shit had been fully eradicated.

Well, out of bed and into the day. Booth pulls up his Levis and finds his shoes under the sofa. See this house with a flood of daylight, doorways arched and with cut glass panes giving off rainbows and halos.

—m—

On the following Monday morning, to be sure he got off on the right foot, Booth dialed the number Tuck had given him. A woman's voice answered.

"May I speak to Tuck please?"

A pause on the other end. "You mean Tucker?"

"Uh, yeah, ok. Guitar player?"

"He's not here anymore."

"No? Um. Know where I can reach him?"

"You can try Lonnie's house. I don't know the number, though."

"Do you know where Lonnie lives?"

"Somewhere on the West Bank. Gretna, maybe."

"Ok, thanks."

Turns to Jill. "That's a bummer. Looks like Tuck disappeared. Unless you happen to know someone named Lonnie, who lives somewhere on the West Bank. Gretna, maybe."

Jill was washing dishes. "Really?" She placed a cup in the drainer. "Sure you dialed it right?"

"Pretty sure. Sounded like an ex-girlfriend. Or wife."

"Well, you can ask Cole when he gets home. He might know this Lonnie."

"Where'd he go?"

"Said he had some business uptown. He mentioned something about some pot. I don't really ask him too many questions, Wesley." She paused. "Did I tell you we're having a party Saturday night?"

"Saturday? Oh, well, great. It'll give me some time to get some writing in. And to find Tuck."

Jill smiles a little smile and raises her eyebrows. "I think Lenna's going to be here."

"Oh, really. Well that'll be cool, huh? But I guess she'll have her fella with her, right?"

"I don't think so. I just talked to her a little on the phone, and she didn't sound real happy."

"Oh yeah? How come?" Booth lights a Winston.

Jill hangs up the dish towel, stretching it neatly across the towel rack. "I think she's disenchanted with Bobby."

That afternoon, Jill away at Tulane, teaching an introductory course in Western Civilization. Andries sitting with legs crossed on the floor, sealing up bricks of marijuana in Reynold's Wrap. An agricultural scent of peppered grass in the air. Booth uneasy, as though the smell could be detected all over the neighborhood. Mentioning this possibility to Andries.

"Booth, you've got the weirdest fucking ideas I ever heard. What do you think, they've got the place under some kind of *smell* surveillance? Shit, we just got here."

"Just trying to cover all the weasel holes. I heard once about this guy that..."

*BRRRRNG!*

"Catch that, man, will you?"

A voice on the other end. "Cole there?"

A Friday morning, days gone by with no word from Tuck, but Booth filled with resolve to push this writing thing into action. Become a man of letters. He began:

> *Eleven year old Willis Bowen sat with his arms wrapped around his knees and watched the last candle burn down. The portable radio had faded to silence, broken only by the flares of static which accompanied the frequent lightning. He picked up the radio and unsnapped the leather case, twisting the batteries like he'd seen his uncle do several hours ago, as he drunkenly tried to get a hurricane update.*

Just standing up for a stretch. Going well here; a good story line. The right touch of drama to pique the interest of a publisher, send me an advance. Someone with vision and able to recognize talent when he sees it. I've heard of writers receiving boxcar loads of rejection slips before they were published. However, to continue...

*Willis held the speaker to his ear and listened into the rustling blackness as hard as he could, finger plugging his other ear against the wind screaming outside the storm windows. He twisted the tuner slowly back and forth, searching for a station.*

There's a kink in my neck. Tension caused by the mind working vigorously. It's perfectly normal, I'm sure. I'm here alone. Jill gone to Schwegmann's to load up on party supplies. Andries just out, as is normal. A pleasant day outside, as long as I'm inside. Haven't checked, but I'll bet there is heat and humidity out there. H&H, the thing that keeps me a recluse, tethered to the air conditioner. And, of course, this writing. Sit me back down.

*Finally, he put the radio down and returned to staring at the candle, letting his cramped legs dangle off the poker table. He tried to imagine that he was safe in Houston with his mother, but something touched his toe in the darkness. He yanked his foot up and peered over the edge of the table.*

Well, writing or not, I've got to piss. Standing in front of the toilet, bare feet on black and white tiles, a powerful stream churning up froth. Shake it off and put it away. Wash the hands if in a public place. There's a law about that for cooks and busboys. Doesn't apply to writers.

A walk around the inside of the house. Feel a little guilty in Andries and Jill's room, but it's necessary for the full experience. The bed nicely made, a quilt and the brass bedstead. Mirrored dresser with a lace doily and framed pictures of the two of them. Small collection of perfume bottles, tiny and delicate. The underwear drawer, a lucky first try. Pulling out a sample. Ooh, peach colored bikinis.

And underneath, my eyes blinking at a private trove, a corpulent stack of money in a rubber band. And Andries' voice instantly in my mind like a revolver cocking. The unforgivable intrusion discovered. Ignore it, picking up the cash to count it. Quickly through the roll like a card shark, fat greasy fifties and hundreds, a total of eight thousand, three hundred fifty. My word.

Booth peels off a fifty, thinks about it for a moment, then stretches the rubber band back into circumference and puts the stack back where it was. More poking, and finds another. Then two more.

Cover it all back up and get out of here.

Ominously, a letter arrives, forwarded unopened by Booth's mother. Booth opens it the way one lets a captured cottonmouth out of the bag. Here's what it says:

Law Offices of
**EDMUND PETERS**
a Professional Corporation

2298 Murray Street
Alexandria, Louisiana 71360
(318) 971-3526

September 7, 1971

Mr. Wesley Booth
c/o Mrs. Thelma Booth
501 Donahue Ferry Rd.
Pineville, La. 71360

Dear Mr. Booth:

This letter is in regard to an incident on or about September 1 of this year involving the theft and/or destruction of property belonging to Ozark Distributing, Inc., a company headquartered in Pine Bluff Ark.

We would like to meet with you in our offices to take your deposition of facts relevant to the foregoing matter. We have discovered certain inconsistencies in the information given to Robert Malone, your employer, the night of September 1 last, when compared to evidence gathered by Grant and Rapides Parish sheriff's deputies.

Specifically, you stated to Mr. Malone that you were robbed, and in fact abducted, during the course of your work at I.A. Gimble Mercantile in Jena, La. This is at some variance with statements taken from witnesses in Jena that afternoon. For example, Mrs. Modine Gimble, the owner of Gimble Mercantile, states that she saw you drive the van away from her store in a reckless manner. In fact, she goes so far as to state that you seemed to be intoxicated during the discharge of your responsibilities at her establishment on September 1.

Further, you stated to Mr. Malone that the alleged assailants had set fire to the merchandise belonging to said Company. The investigating deputies state that not only the merchandise but in fact the delivery van itself, a 1970 Ford Econoline, was destroyed by fire.

Of considerably more interest to law enforcement officials here was the fact that the vehicle had been perforated by gunfire. A number of projectiles, in calibers .38 and .45, were recovered at the scene. Deputies stated that this revealed a wanton element not usually encountered in vandalism cases in Central Louisiana. They have a high level of interest in apprehending the suspects, and since you were in the employ of Ozark Distributing at the time of the incident, I have been instructed to inform you of Ozark's desire that you cooperate fully with law enforcement officials in this regard.

Please contact us at your earliest convenience to arrange an appointment. We are sure you will want to clear this matter up as soon as possible.

Very truly yours,
Edmund H. Peters

A vexing thought occurs to Booth: How did she know where to send it? Did some kind of cosmic tendril slither its way back there? A filament of filial fetter?

He winds a blank page into the typewriter. A quick note to put this thing to rest forever:

*Dear Mr. Peters:*

*It is with deep sadness and regret that I inform you of the untimely passing of my son Wesley. According to the reports I have received, he was mistaken for an alligator and shot several times while he was resting near a roadway in Calcasieu Parish. The sheriff's department is conducting a full investigation, but as I'm sure you are aware, the people down there are rather primitive and prone to...*

A knock at the door.

"Uh huh," still involved with the writing. The door opening with characteristic scrape, and in walks Jill.

"How's your writing going?"

"Oh, OK. Just a little passage about reptiles. Crocodilians..." Pulling out the fraudulent missive to avoid discovery.

"Still no luck in finding those musicians? Tuck?"

"No. I asked Cole, but he didn't have any leads."

"Well, I need to talk to you a little. I don't want you to take this the wrong way, but Cole has asked me a couple of times now what your plans are."

"My plans?" Booth looks for his cigarettes, nervously. "Well, I'm still looking for Tuck, and I expect I'll track him down eventually."

"Mmmm. I think it's the eventually part that's bothering Cole a little. Have you driven out to that club in Metairie they were talking about?"

"No, it wasn't really clear to me which one they meant. Of course, meanwhile, there's my writing. I've got a really good feeling about this current batch."

Jill pauses, then smiles. "Well good, then. Just a word to the wise, ok?"

Booth watches her back with sideways eyes as she returns toward the kitchen. Gets up and stretches. Walks into the kitchen. "I think I'll pop down to Lemoine's and pick up a paper or two. They might have some info on the bands playing around here. Might find Tuck, and even if I don't, there's gotta be some other stuff happening."

Jill smiles. "That's a good idea, Wesley. I just bet you're right."

"Can I bring something back for you?"

## eight

# *malagueña*

From a claustrophobic position in the kitchen, Booth looks out on this scene:

There are something like thirty people compressed into convivial intimacy in the several rooms of the house. Smoke and glib conversations lofted up in marijuana bubbles to the arched corners of the room. The police could have a field day here, arresting and clubbing these miscreants. I can't see why people want to seek these little thrills. Always pushing things, crossing lines and tweaking the noses of Minotaurs, or monitors. But if there was a raid, I could escape through a window and fade into the night. Exchange a few words with the officers on the folly of it all, go on my merry way, clutching my thoroughly legal beverage.

Booth swigs from his second bottle of wine of the evening and in a mood to talk about the way things were. He is backed up to the kitchen counter, with two people talking eagerly toward him.

But just now Lenna walks in, wearing a dark skirt and white bolero blouse. A throb of lust in Booth's chest as he watches her pick a path through the crowd. A distracted look on her face, however, and Booth can't catch her eye. She immediately disappears with Jill into the bedroom.

Well, back to this conversation, then. A man and his wife, both of them teachers. The woman offers an opinion to Booth:

"It seems to me that the Pentagon has become the oracle of modern American philosophy."

"The Pentagon? May I ask what you're talking about?"

A few minutes later, Jill comes out of the bedroom. Lenna follows in a moment, sits down on the sofa, looking a bit lost. She is immediately surrounded by several men who begin vying in the most obvious and annoying way for her attention.

The teacher makes her point clear:

"Well, I think that people should just be able to get along with each other."

Booth looks at her for a moment, then asks her a pointed question:

"But where does that leave our defense posture?" I find this woman's attitude very irritating. "Holly...that was your name, wasn't it? I mean what are your thoughts on that?"

Her librarian eyes bulging wet like marbles under their hooded lids. Pekingese eyes behind Catwoman glasses. A sharp rap to the back of the head and out they'd pop. Just kidding. Booth lights a cigarette, a blue burr of Zippo flame. Snapped shut and dropped into his shirt pocket. Studying the woman closely. A clearing of the throat by her husband, nervously, and looking away, finding compelling interest in the construction of a macramé plant hanger.

The teacher's black hair was bobbed squarely in the back, a handbag clutched under the arm. "Exactly how do you mean?" Delicate glass of pink wine grasped by her soft schoolmarm hand.

Another glance through the crowd to see a man light a joint and hand it roguishly to Lenna.

"I mean exactly how do you feel about the military? Do you feel that our motives were wrong?"

"Which motives were those?"

"Stopping the spread of communism. Plain as day."

A smile of uneasy condescension. "Oh come now." She looked around. "You don't really *believe* that, do you?"

"I do. I believe what our president says. I believe we're in danger."

*"Oh, really."* Looking around for support, her husband vanished toward the icebox after beer. "Do you mean *Nixon?*"

"Indeed I do. He's the president, isn't he? Now I'd like to hear what you think about our foreign policy. America's policy is the one I'm talking about." Booth paused. "You're aware that I was wounded in battle, aren't you?"

See Lenna drawing at the joint, missing my gaze as she hands it back. Booth turns his attention back to the teacher. His wrist tipping up the bottle of wine, like Popeye with his spinach. In fact, now that I take notice, this woman looks quite a lot like Olive Oyl. Could stand to lose a bit of weight, though, to achieve the full effect. Needs that little sausage-like pigtail, too. Now a scholarly man squeezing brazenly into the space next to Lenna on the couch.

Booth, speaking again to the teacher, who seems to be edging away:

"Listen, never mind about that political stuff. I was just kidding, anyway." He drew close, conspiratorially. "What I'd really like to know was whether Olive Oyl was exclusively Popeye's woman or if Bluto was fucking her too. If you can imagine such a thing." He laughed lightly. "I mean, I find it a little hard to tell who's who in those cartoons, don't you? Their relationships, I mean. All those twists and turns in the plot. I was thinking you might have a special perspective on the thing." A rapt look of attention on her frozen face.

Now Andries intervening from the periphery, wearing an unfamiliar and sneaky face of pacifist.

"Booth, are you bothering the guests again? Ma'am, I hope you'll forgive Wesley."

"Well, really, I thought maybe I'd said something wrong."

"No, no, you were just fine. Things have been a little rough for him lately, that's all. Jill should probably have mentioned it to you."

Leading Booth away, arm around the neck. "Trying to get in her britches, dude? Hey, if you're looking to get laid, and who's not, right, why not try Spot? Jill said she's bummed about some shit. Go cheer her up."

"Spot?" Booth's eyebrows up.

"Lenna, man. You didn't see that thing under her arm? Scared the shit out of me, buddy."

"Oh, that." The birthmark. A small and uncomfortable feeling of malice implied here.

Andries' half drunken leer. "Never know, man. Could be her whole tit's that color. Wouldn't that be the shits? Hey, and Jill said Lenna thinks you're nice, too, man. Are you nice?" He laughed harshly and lit a joint. "Spot." He repeated, turning away. "That tickles my ass, man."

Booth back into the kitchen for a proper wine glass, twisting carefully in the kitchen crowd. Then tediously to the refrigerator. Permission to pass here, please. By your leave, sir. What sort of squealing cataclysm would follow if I seized the testicles of one of this pack of intellectuals in my talons, jammed as they are into this small space, talking about unusual topics. He pulls a bottle of Mateus out of the refrigerator, pours it into the glass.

On his way back, Jill turns from a conversation. "Oh, Wesley. Do you think you could go up to Lemoine's and get some more chips and stuff? I really underestimated." An innocent look. "Maybe Lenna'd like to take a walk with you. She just had a fight with Bobby and she's a little down right now." She handed him a ten dollar bill in a casual way and returned to her conversation.

Lenna sitting on the print, corduroy sofa, pinioned by that bespectacled man with sweater and paisley tie, and him talking in a proprietary way. Eyebrows like caterpillars and thin hair arcing foppishly from the temples. Booth approaches from the back, holding the glass of Mateus around in front of Lenna's nose, making her start back and look around.

"Oh, it's you. Hello again." She took the glass, pulled her black skirt back down. See relief on her face, amongst a collection of emotions. "Gumby, if I recall."

The man next to her commented rather sourly that they were having a conversation, which they were not.

Booth responds: "Are you taking umbrage, sir?" Then, to Lenna, "It never fails to amuse me when people take umbrage. And that's what I feel is happening right now, don't you?" He stuck his nose into the man's face. The Dagwood head recoiling.

"I think you should understand that the umbrage you were planning on taking belongs to this young lady right here. You can't have it. I don't mean to seem abrupt, but sometimes it's best to be direct." A look of fear in the man's eyes. "Anyway, someone in the kitchen was looking for you. I believe it was your wife. She had that look about her anyway–a lumpish woman, with a scarf on her head." The man getting up slowly, so as not to give evidence of having been railroaded. But leaving nonetheless, his tie drunkenly askew. Booth looking at Lenna with a happy smile.

"That was mean," she said. But the eyes making the beginnings of a smile.

"Here, I'll call him back..." Booth rising to yodel after the man. Lenna yanking him back down by the arm. "Don't you dare. He was just a dirty old man."

"I could have him killed if you like. I know some people in the mob." He shook a Winston out of the red and white pack. Snapped off the filter and offered it to Lenna.

Looking up at Booth's remembered eccentricity. Taking the cigarette. "Aren't you ever serious?"

Down on his knees, his chin on the back of the sofa. "I gave it a try once, Lenna, that serious business. But some people took it the wrong way and the next thing I knew I had been set upon by assailants."

"My eyes are burning. Do they look red?" Her face upturned for examination within a delicate billow of smoke.

Booth squinting closely as she rolled them around, big green eyes and lashes to spare. Girls have them more abundantly than we do. A nice thing too, engineered to do that thing they're doing to me right now. Make me respond in a certain way that will further the evolutionary goals of the race. I'll have to say that there are some manipulations I don't mind. That slight overbite causing a wuthering pulse of lust. And her neck curved in this presenting way...

"Well, are they red?"

"Uh, yes. They are just a bit bloodshot. All this smoke and chattering. Would you like to get a breath of fresh air? If you don't find it annoying, we could walk down to Lemoine's. It's just about two blocks away. I need to pick up some shoe polish anyway."

"But you don't have any shoes on."

Looking back, his heels washed pink. "You're right. Good of you to mention it. I'll pick up a pair while we're out. On credit." He stood up slowly with a grimace. Lenna's hand went to his arm in a show of concern.

"Are you OK? That's right, Jill said something about your leg. Will you be able to walk?"

"It's nothing, really. Just a little schrapnel I picked up in Vietnam. Gets stiff sometimes. The walk'll do me good."

Negotiating their way through the jabbering crowd, out the back door into the swaddling broth of New Orleans at midnight. The organic tongue of the South, lapping fleshly at the armpit.

Booth walking, barefoot, next to the street, swinging a branch torn from the crepe myrtle tree in front of the house, bottle of Boone's Farm pending from the left knuckles. A welter of insects overhead, a seething cloud bright around the mercury vapor streetlamp. Some of the less fortunate ones here on the sidewalk, wounded and underfoot from flying too close to the siren envelope of white-hot plasma.

"Where do you come from, Lenna? Are you an American?" A cockroach the length of a thumb fled madly across the sidewalk. Booth poked at it with the stick, altering its primal, brainless course.

"I'm from London. England."

"Ah, a subject of the Crown. And this boyfriend you're having trouble with...is he an immigrant of some sort?"

A laugh in spite of the audacity. "Oh for God's sake. You say the queerest things. You met him in Alexandria that night. We just had a disagreement, that's all. He's not really a bad person, but he can get quite angry."

"What was the fight about?"

"Oh, just a long story. I think he was a mistake."

"He clearly has a troubled ego. I take it that you live with this person."

"Well, about three months now."

A carload of teenagers passed by, the radio turned up to an unintelligible tinkling squall. Booth sighed. "I suppose it won't work out then."

"What won't work out?"

"Well, I'd hoped to interest you in coming to Nebraska with me, but I can see that you're already spoken for."

A pause, uncertain. "Take me to Nebraska? Why are you going there?"

"It's a little research project. A grant. Tornado research."

"Tornadoes?"

"I'm going to reap the whirlwind, Lenna."

She shook her head. "Jill did say you were different. You don't even know me, really." She adjusted her blouse with an unconsciously provocative movement, her breasts rising, resettling.

"But I can tell that your faith is strong, Lenna. Jethro Tull does a song about that. Faith, I mean." Booth unscrews the cap from the bottle of Boone's Farm, offers it to Lenna. She takes a polite sip.

Booth continues: "And don't we all really know each other? I mean, we're all little waves on the same pond, aren't we?"

"Waves on a pond? What are you on about now?" Lenna looks at him dubiously, but with a smile just the same.

"The pond of the universe, Lenna, the pond of essence, the firmament. Surely you learned about that in church."

"Twaddle. I was raised atheist."

"I'm not talking about religion, Lenna. I'm talking about the ether that connects us. The filaments. The tendrils. Unless maybe you believe in that singularity business. The Big Bang?"

"Please, Wesley. I did go to university."

"So did I. Just ask Jill."

"Jill told me you were ejected."

"That's not true. I withdrew as a matter of principle."

"Jill said the principle was your French professor's wife."

"I was the target of a smear, a whispering campaign. Which I admit sounds better in *français* than in English. American English, anyway. Something about that uvular trill. And let's not forget, I was young and innocent back then. I was a victim of predation."

"Predation indeed." But I can see that smile again.

Booth makes an appalling attempt at a British accent. "Lenna, you're quite the fetching lass. If you don't find it irritating that I noticed."

She laughed. "Was that your strategy then, to irritate me?"

"No, I just thought that your boyfriend might have a problem with me noticing ... what was his name again?"

"Bobby."

"I thought so. A lot of trouble with those people, Lenna, a lot of trouble. That's where the term came from. For cops, I mean."

"Be nice, now. Jill said you were nice. A bit queer, but nice."

"I'd like to be remembered as a kindly person, Lenna. I always try to act that way. It does have the disadvantage of attracting the wrong people sometimes, though. Beggars, that sort. The feeble. By the way, you want to be careful with that term "queer." These illiterates here in the colonies only know one meaning for it."

"Oh, indeed."

"Say, Jill tells me you used to associate with some gods of your own. Rock stars."

"Yeah, a bit. Not rock stars, really. I was on the periphery. I was engaged to Jordan Witte."

"Don't know him."

"You wouldn't. But he was involved in managing tours for some of the big acts from England, and I traveled on a few excursions."

"Wow, impressive. Which bands?"

"Oh, Jethro Tull, The Who, Cat Stevens, The Kinks. Quite a list, really."

"Stones?"

"No, but I met them once or twice. Oh, and Zeppelin."

"For real? Man. So how is it you're in New Orleans, chatting with the likes of me?"

"The likes of you?" Lenna sighed. "That's rather a longer story. But the short version is that Jordan was yet another mistake. So I went over the side last year during a swing through New Orleans."

A thunderhead flared suddenly through the trees to the west, a tightly clotted mass of menace, the color of a marauding shark.

Lenna came closer and her arm touched his. "Oooh. Looks like we might be in for a bit of a blow."

Booth picked up the pace. "We're in for it, Lenna." He unscrewed the bottle cap, took another pull. A few seconds later came the bump of thunder.

At 1:36 in the morning, his hair still damp from the rain, Booth is playing the Les Paul at the request of the several who remained. The ember of a joint made arcs in the dark. Having been persuaded to partake of the pot, his fingers traced a furious rendition of the *Malagueña*. Meanwhile, Jill and Lenna, who had changed into frilly black skirts from Jill's cedar chest, struck a *flamenco* tattoo upon the oak floor with their dainty boots. Holly, the philosophy teacher, enraptured and drunk, had to be restrained by her husband from disrobing.

Booth worked the music down to a drone in E, then finished with an A harmonic minor run from the top all the way down to the nut. The girls made a final stamp and flourish with their boots and skirts, after which Lenna slid down the wall to light beside Booth, radiating waves of girl-scented heat. Her hand came over and rested on Booth's forearm.

Later that night, find Booth with his back against the wall, his feeble protests of uprightness under savage attack by Lenna.

I've heard or rather read that men prefer to take the lead in this situation, but the truth is that I'll take it any way I can get it. As cleverly as a swain if possible, but yielding if that's the way it's going to be, as in this case of Lenna stripping off my sheet with a panting whine that I'm sure must be audible to Andries and Jill through the adjoining bathroom. I always wonder with a detached part of my mind about the thoughts others must have, since it seems to be true that everybody does it, each in their own way.

Forcing his way out of the corner, hand twined in her hair, tongues touching in that explicit way, her blouse pulled up roughly. See these rounded breasts, nipples erect in the street-light window frame. On her knees and me on mine, this play of ancient passion throbbing to rupture in the small hours of the New Orleans night. Now these panties, her breath a whistling moan. My hand cupping this incomparably soft and smooth nether curve under transcendent frilly wisp of silk, a provoked ascending sob in my ear.

"Caution, Lenna, caution. We'll wake up the neighbors and their little brown dog."

Oh, the shape of hips, and the shadow of navel above that cleft triangle of empyrean madness with panties half down. Touching lightly in my bold manner. And my head filled with girlscent, pushing me to excess in squeezing so that I'm mindful of hurting, although she seems to favor it. A flurry of position-ing in this tiny bed, sheet tangled around the foot. Brief frantic struggle and free, touching now that place of supreme privacy, her neck arched back and trembling, tongue touching this upright nipple. See her lips open, now teeth pulling up bottom lip, the chin thrust forward. Nostrils and those eyes and lashes, designed for this purpose exactly, even in the dark causing my rutting pulse to quicken to a hammering thump. Now wrestling her easily onto her back in this squawking little bed, panties slipped off in a quick sweep and airborne, as she raised her hips to help with a magically willing spirit. It needs to be said that I never quite believe it when I find myself in this clutch, no matter how many times it's been before.

Now encouraging me into the classical configuration with her toes pointed at the ceiling in an acrobatic fashion, kissing my chest and neck with panting suckling lips. And the moment of truth coming just moments later, embarrassingly, in a spasmodic humping rictus, spine like a scorpion's tail, checkerboard flashes across my blinded vision. Rocked by aftershocks so intense that Lenna asks if I'm all right, big British eyes wide with concern.

Now a thump on the wall and Andries' vulgar laugh from the next room. "Hey Booth. What color was it? Same as the other one?" Followed by a slap from Jill and exclaiming "*Cole!*" in an offended tone, then her own muffled giggling.

Me collapsing on Lenna, her fingers in my sweaty hair.

In the morning, Booth wakes up and smells the coffee. He can also smell Lenna's hair. From the sounds in the kitchen Andries and Jill are up and about and there's the smell of bacon. Lenna squirms closer. Her eyebrow touches his chin. He plants a small kiss on her forehead. His hand wanders down under the sheet, gliding along her left hip with a smooth but thrilling correspondence, something more religion than lust. As close as

Booth figures he'll get to the angels, singing that chorus of deliverance in 5-part harmony.

—◆—

On Sunday, Booth and Lenna visit the Audubon Zoo. In an atmosphere charged with feral stinks, African grunts and Amazon screeches, Lenna asks a simple question. "When you were on the other night about going to Nebraska you weren't actually serious, were you?"

Booth turns his thoughtful, fibbing face. "Well…"

"…because Jill mentioned that you don't like nasty weather."

Booth pauses, points a finger into the air, and spills a quote:

*My life is cold, and dark, and dreary;*
*It rains, and the wind is never weary;*

"I believe Longfellow wrote that little ditty, so maybe I'm in good company…"

In her turn, Lenna purses her lips, then, "Yes, but didn't he also write:"

*Be still, sad heart, and cease repining;*
*Behind the clouds is the sun still shining;*

Booth's eyes slide sideways toward Lenna. Who looks back with a face of innocent challenge.

He starts to open his mouth, but is saved further literary maneuvers by a developing outrage around the hippopotamus pool. People were scrambling away with screaming horrified mouths.

When the crowd had cleared, Booth had an unobstructed view of the river horse's gigantic arse hoisted a foot above the brown surface of the water, the tail oscillating like a one-bladed ceiling fan, flinging ordure over the hippo fence in a 30 foot arc. A score of zoo-goers, aghast and gagging, scraping green clods and drizzles off their Sunday best. One unfortunate woman, a Baptist by all appearances, cast her befouled hat away in horror.

Skirting this holocaust by a circuitous route, Booth and Lenna arrive at a chorus of siamang gibbons, honking and barking away the Sabbath with their gray bubble gum throats.

Lenna repeats, "So, Nebraska?"

"Ah, I was just kidding. Actually, I'd like to see the west. Flagstaff, maybe."

"Yes, I've seen pictures. What would you plan to do out there?"

Booth takes a breath, considers his next lie carefully. Breathes out an evasion. "Plan...?"

"No idea, then?" Lenna looks at his face. "No real strategy in mind?"

Here Booth hoots back at the huddled assembly of simians, who fall momentarily silent, seeming to sense a certain brotherhood. "I kind of like to keep my options open, if you know what I mean."

"I see." Lenna looks at him. "And that seems to be working? I mean, you're obviously an excellent guitarist. What options are you looking at with that, if you don't mind me asking?"

Booth ducks his head. An inquest here. "Do I have the right to remain silent? Jeez..."

Lenna smiles. "Of course. This is America, isn't it? You can have a lawyer present, if you wish."

Booth casts a British inflection. "My barrister's offices are in Alexandria." Still waiting for an explanation of that smoking, bullet-ravaged husk of Ford van in the woods up there, I expect. I wonder if he's looked into the possibility of spontaneous combustion, or a lightning strike?

"And you have plans, then? Do you plan to work at Tulane until your spinsterhood?"

"I plan to work there until I save enough money to get to Seattle."

"Seattle?" Booth stops. A lowland gorilla gazes with bored countenance from the corner of its cage. "What's in Seattle?"

"Some friends from London live there. They're trying to start a small music label. In fact, it's very small right now. But Barb, my friend, wrote a couple of months back and offered me an opportunity with them."

"I was there once, Seattle. Rains a lot, but I'll have to say that it's quite a bit cooler than Louisiana." Booth shakes out two Winstons. Pinches the filter off of one and hands it to Lenna. Her hand with plain-cut fingernails cups his as he lights it.

A pivotal question. "What about Bobby?"

Lenna french inhales the white smoke. "Well, there is that, isn't there?"

"Wesley, we've got a spot of bother here."

Booth comes out of Bobby's house and there are those very muttonchops, right here on the front porch. Raising his voice at Lenna. Reaching for her as she backs away, arms around a stuffed bullfrog. Jeremiah, with a happy smile and tongue sticking out. Booth takes Bobby by his double-knit jacket sleeve and spins him around. Bobby raises an aggressive hand. Booth drops his shopping bag of clothes and seizes Bobby by the hair on his cheeks. "Ah ah, sir. Let's all be grownups now..."

Bobby jerks his face away, tottering back down a couple of the porch steps. But he lowers his hand. "*What the fuck is this? This is my house.* What are you doing, babe?"

Booth speaks up. "Lenna has found greener pastures, if you'll indulge a metaphor. A nest with finer down, as it were. Lenna also has a key to this house. These are her things in this bag. I don't want to appear churlish, but the fact has to be faced that you've been found wanting, sir." Bobby makes a face at Lenna above his fat gold tie, but then his eyes nervously looking back at Booth.

Booth picks up the bag. "Well. We'll just be on our way, then."

Three days later, the four of them sitting around the dinner table, scavenging the fricasseed remnants of shrimp tacos from floral plates. The phone rings. Andries says, "Can you reach that, Booth?"

Booth reaches back, lifts the yellow wall phone receiver. "Yellow?"

A man's voice says, "Cole there, please?"

Andries takes the phone, stretches the long curly cord around the corner into the living room. Booth continues with an explication of his wave theory, prompting a challenge from Lenna:

"Ok, then, if you're a wave, or a ripple as you say, what happens when you die? You just disappear, right? Or do you go to wave heaven?"

Booth counters: "Does the water in a wave evaporate when the wave collapses? Where do the actual molecules go?"

"So your point is that the soul is composed of molecules? Really, Wesley?"

"No, I'm making an analogy here." Booth opens another beer. Gives Lenna a wry smile. "Besides, why is an atheist defending the soul?"

"I'm certainly not. I was questioning the basis for your analogy."

Andries comes back in, hangs up the phone. Stands by the back door, silently watching this existential debate, with a pensive, distant look on his stone age features. After a bit of his face, the table falls silent. Andries lets it marinate for a minute, then asks a favor.

"Booth, reckon you can give me a hand with something tomorrow? Pretty early."

"Uh, sure."

Andries turns the doorknob, opens the door, letting in a wave of humidity. Looks around with a look that passed through everybody.

"I'll be back in a little bit, babe."

# nine

## *rest stop*

Seven o'clock AM on the following morning, as plain a Thursday as ever there was, see Booth riding shotgun, eastward in Andries' GTO on US 90. The Les Paul in the back seat, along with an ice chest containing beer. In the trunk, five cardboard tubes that Andries got out of the laundry room back of the garage.

Andries seems tense, preoccupied. He says this:

"I'm gonna let you in on a little secret, Booth. Just in case you see something you don't expect to see. Those tubes back there? Those ain't fly rods or posters. You remember hearing about an art heist at that museum here a few months back? No? Well, there's a couple hundred grand worth of old paint and canvas back there in my trunk. I guess they were waiting for everything to go cold before they moved the shit."

"What? Shit," says Booth. "You did that?"

"Hell no. All I know about art is which one is Mona and which one is Lisa. I'm just muling the shit, making the handoff."

"You expecting some kind of trouble over here?"

"Nah, money guys never want that kind of shit. But I don't know this guy, so better safe than sorry."

"Um. What do you want me to do?"

"Do? You won't need to do anything. Just be cool. It's just a matter of having two people instead of one."

"Like a psychological advantage?"

Andries, looks over. "Uh, yeah, like that."

"Alright, cool. You mind me asking how you got hold of the paintings? I don't mean to pry, but that's a lot of jail time back there."

"Let's just say I know some people I probably shouldn't. They asked me to haul this shit over and bring back the bread. Actually, it was Mike that put them in touch with me. He's the bike guy calls himself Chain, remember from the party up there? That's one of the things you might see."

*8:38 AM*

Just west of Bay St. Louis, Mississippi, Andries pulled the GTO into a magnolia-shrouded rest area. Stopping near the brick restrooms. And there are the three Harleys parked in a line, the riders smoking cigarettes, obviously waiting. A dark green Ford also there, door open, a man at the wheel.

An uncomfortable flash of recollection: "Yo, there they are."

"Yeah." Andries' eyes intent as he pulled the car to a stop, adjusting something on the floor with his left foot. "Listen, why don't you go take it easy for a few minutes. Stretch your legs. Have a beer. I've just got a little business to transact here." He paused. "Um, hey...lock that door when you get out, OK? Be sure, now."

Booth took his guitar and a fresh can of beer from the back seat. Got out and locked the door as instructed. As he stepped away from the car, Redbone fixed him with a flat stare and said, "Guitar man. Brought your own beer this time?" Just ignore him, a nod and a smile to acknowledge. Glance at the driver of the Ford. Older guy, balding.

Walk over to this gray concrete picnic table. I really wish I wasn't here, to be perfectly honest. I hope Andries hasn't got us into God knows what. Headlines tomorrow of two killed savagely in the peaceful shade of a Mississippi roadside rest area, motive unknown.

Booth mounts the table casually, hoping to still the aura of dread he felt himself radiating. Look with veiled eyes and Andries could be seen talking in an offhand way with the other three. Birds made their sounds in the trees. The driver of the Ford gets out, removes a large paper bag from the back seat. Hands it to Andries.

After a few minutes, there was an upraising of voices, and Booth lifts his head nervously to see. But then reason apparently reasserted itself, and the bikers could be seen listening intently to Andries. They conferred for another minute, then all walked toward the Pontiac. The near side, the door Booth had made sure to lock. Andries tried the handle nonetheless, then could be heard to mutter "Shit, fucking Booth locked it. Hang on and I'll open it up." He walks around and opens the driver's door, stepping with easy purpose. The bikers fan out, triangulating the GTO. Andries drops the bag into the back seat, bends deep inside the car. The trunk lid pops open, drawing the attention of the three.

Now Andries stands up, starkly, with the .45 automatic in his hand, and the machined *clank* of the slide pulled and released. Pointing over the car and the bikers backing away with hands raised up, a circumstance suddenly turned. Booth steps off the table, then *POW!* See Chain dropping to his knees with squealing mouth of pain and fear.

A cloud of sparrows exploded out of the trees above Booth, winging it in terror. Andries swung the gun toward the one at the front of the car, who was attacking in a desperate rush. He had the good fortune that the .45 had jammed. And also that he weighed about 40 pounds more than Andries. Andries grabbed the slide with his right hand and yanked. He was left-handed and had to turn to face the biker. The man grabbed the wrist of Andries' gun hand in the bare nick of time and the .45 went off in mid swing. The bullet, randomly projected, could be heard to ricochet with a Western whine off of something high and behind Booth. A seed pod from the overhanging magnolia dropped with a thunk onto the table beside him.

Booth could see the gun clearly as the focus of the struggle, held desperately away in Andries' fist and scrabbled for by the other while he sought a fatal grip on Andries' throat. On hands and knees, Chain scuttled with a surprising but doomed haste toward the front of the car before going nose down, then half rising and rolling onto his back.

Booth approached at a middling speed, tethered by fear of what would happen if he got there before Andries resolved the situation, but prodded by the need to show willingness to help. As he arrived at the body of Chain, he saw movement, but not hope; there was a blue hole just below the man's collarbone and a rivulet of blood coursed from the corner of his mouth, dripping from the gold ring in his left ear down to a small puddle in the dust. There was a look of inward disgust on his pinched-shut eyes. Still, Booth feared he might suddenly revive and grab his ankle.

Booth made a hair-raising hop, and at the inescapable end of his walk he saw the driver of a east-bound semi looking unmistakably in their direction, brown cab, baseball cap and sunshades. Understanding finally that reason or discussion would not set things right, Booth took the Les Paul's neck in both hands, down by the tuning head.

His swing would have scored at least a Little League homer, and the solid body of the guitar glanced off the man's shoulder before connecting edgewise with the right occipital lobe of his head. Insanely, Booth remembered reading in the Warren Report that this was the same chunk that was blown off a former president's cranium a few years back.

A detail was clear: the biker's right triceps relaxed as though he had changed his mind about the fight, possibly guided by a surge of good will. Then he dropped like a bag of offal, sliding helplessly down the front of Andries, whose neck still bore a white thumb print.

Booth heard the staccato rattle of jake brakes up the road to the east. Andries pushed away from the car, kicking the man off his knees, and directed a terrible focus toward Redbone, who, thirty feet away, was fumbling desperately with something on the far side of his bike. He backed away from the bike immediately at Andries' approach and put his palms out in front, eyes wide and mouth imploring, making sounds. See his supplicant demeanor with bandana shaken loose and sticking up playfully. Booth sees a stain spread darkly down the left leg of his sullied jeans.

But just the same, Andries, his face like the Reaper taunted, raises the gun and *POW!* See the gun jump abruptly up in recoil, the blast jerking dust out of the biker's clothes and his hair snapping back, bandana flying off. The ejected cartridge spun high over Andries' shoulder in a flashing golden arc. Redbone dropped to his knees, arms limp, then forward, his head cradled in the lowslung saddle of the Harley. The fat .45 shell clinked onto the gravel.

Now Andries back toward the car, motioning with the pistol to hurry up. The guitar-whacked man was trying to get up, making a horrible attempt to smile, as if this whole thing was merely a regrettable mistake that could be put right with a little polite discussion. Andries came up with eyes like a wolf. He deliberately circled behind the zombie, taking no chances on the whimsy of the doomed. Booth turned his head away, unable to watch the helpless man die. *POW!* He could feel his own clothes shimmer briefly in the dusty vortex of muzzle blast.

Booth, holding the Les Paul, surveys this scene in a slow-motion take. Andries' GTO parked on the tan gravel. Over there, only 50 feet if I chose to walk it, is the harmless corpse of Redbone, now fallen back away from his bike, lying with legs bent under, arms by his side and face up as though to welcome God or a space visitor.

Now the balding man returning to the Ford, arms around the cardboard tubes from Andries' trunk. There are oak trees and the slick flesh of magnolia leaves, the banana smell of their flowers. Dead boots of that one motorcyclist, whose name I never knew, turned unnaturally askew. I notice the contour and texture of the potholes in the gravel, each small rock in its place. Distinctly, I can hear a squirrel make an exploratory bark. I estimate the temperature to be in the high 80s, maybe 90. The humidity is normal, about 80 percent. The nascent puffs of Gulf clouds that will soon be thunderheads. The liquid sizzle of a car's distant tires on the asphalt. And the grunt of a Diesel engine as, I feel sure, that certain trucker turns his Freightliner around to come investigate. Every molecule is witness to the pestilent waves echoing here, the ears and snouts of the Furies perking up and homing in. The Ford's engine starts and the car turns around. Exits briskly via the east entrance to the rest stop. And although I cannot see him, on the other side of the GTO there is Chain, who told a heroic story once of his life having been saved, deep in a steaming jungle, by a comrade he called the King.

And now there is Andries, having just dragged the corpse of Chain away from the car's path, coming around and shoving something into his belt behind him. Booth gets in the car, slings the Les Paul into the back seat, locks the door.

Andries gets into the driver's seat, twisting the key. A gout of dust and gravel as he stomps on the gas, the car moving sideways and pelting the orphaned Harleys with a fan of gravel. Onto the highway with a long yelp of rubber and Andries spinning the steering wheel to correct away from an oncoming car, its strident Doppler hornbleat receding. Looking back at the tan cloud of dust, the boxy shape of the semi looming in the cloud. Another squawk from the tires as Andries slammed the gearshift into second.

"*Holy fuck. What happened, man?*" Booth could barely hear his own voice.

"*Fucking assholes. You didn't see that gun?* They would have killed us both, sure as hell. I know those fuckers. They were trying to rip off the money and the pictures."

"A gun?...I didn't..."

Andries' wolf eyes burning into Booth's wide ones, spelling things out clearly, as one would to a child.

"At least two of 'em had guns. The one by the bikes almost got to use his. I was damn lucky I saw it in time." He leans forward, reaches behind him, lays a revolver on the seat.

The GTO's speedometer waggled just over a hundred, streaking lawless down this moss draped highway full of smoking terror and death. Acrid smell of oiled steel and smokeless powder. Booth shifts in the seat, and his hand touches the .45 on the console between them. It was undeniably warm. Andries notices and reaches down with one hand, uncocks the gun and dumps the clip. Grips the wheel with his knees and racks the slide, flipping a live round into Booth's lap. A wisp of smoke issues from the breach. Booth reaches around to the ice chest for a beer. Sees a single drop of blood on the bridge pickup of his guitar.

"Shit, man. What are we gonna do now? This is a pretty bad deal, right?" Booth feels an itch in his left wrist, scratches. Then looks down to find blood on the wrist and on his right fingers. Examines the wound, lacerated by the ends of the strings on the tuning head of the guitar. Swallows half the can of Schlitz.

Andries turns with a tight, incredulous grin. "A bad deal? Jesus, Booth, you got a real talent for understatement, you know that? We just *wasted* three guys, in case you didn't notice."

"Don't we have to call the cops or something? It was self defense, right? Pure and simple."

"Cops?" Andries laughed. "Shit, Booth, are you kidding?"

Andries drove straight back toward New Orleans. At one point Booth asks exactly what had happened.

Andries puts it like this:

"You remember those guys, right? Well, they were working for that dude from Atlanta, the money dude. Anyway, I got the word that the Atlanta guy was worried about them trying to pull something, which is why I brought you along. Discourage 'em, you know? Can't say I was expecting this kind of shit, though."

"Oh, man." Booth screws around, reaching into the ice chest for another beer.

"Hey, Booth, you saved my ass back there. I thought you just played that thing."

"I didn't know what else to do, really. This is really fucked up, man. What are we going to do now?"

Andries stops at a McDonald's on the Chef Menteur Highway. Turns around in the seat. "Listen, Booth. Here's the way it is. The cops ain't gonna look very hard for anybody on this. Those guys have been asking for some shit for a long time. They've all got records. The only way I could get snagged is if somebody dropped a nickel on me, and you're the only one that knows anything."

"But what if somebody else saw? Weren't there some other people there? That dude in the other car. I think that truck turned around..."

"Nope. And even if there was, it happened too quick for them to tell anything." He lit up a cigarette. "The guy in the car was the money guy. You don't think they were gonna let him skate, do you?

"Now, this is some serious shit, Booth. I know you never been involved in something like this, but the thing is to just keep quiet, and I mean real fucking quiet. If you were to get scared and go to the cops, or tell somebody that might, that's the end of the road. I'll wind up doing time, or worse, and, frankly, that ain't gonna happen. I don't want this to sound like a threat or anything, cause I know you're not gonna talk." His eyes looking at Booth, to be sure his intent was understood.

"Just remember those assholes didn't get no more than they deserved. Hell, I prob'ly ought to get a commendation. That guy Chain? He did time out in New Mexico for beating the shit out of some little girl." He paused. "One more thing. Don't say anything to Jill, right?"

Oh, the way the ordinary and the fantastically, unspeakably extraordinary meet. Like the intersection of two bubbles. Completely separate, then they touch, unite and become one. Without a sound, bang. Ordinary again.

I remember an unspeakably extraordinary thing that happened ten years ago, when I was thirteen. In a barbershop on Main Street. In the chair with an apron and Kleenex pinned around my neck. And the place busy of a Saturday morning. My hair being cut short on the sides and flat on the top when in walked a man with a burlap bag. A jovial word with the barbers and the five or six other men waiting. Howard and I were the only kids. But I was the one he winked at as he reached into the sack and pulled out the cut off head of a Negro man. He held it up to admire like a new bowling ball.

And I saw the coiled beads of hair on the brown scalp, the eyelids half closed over a faded whiteness and the lips drawn away from dry teeth in an oriental look of sorrow forever. The neck was like jerked beef. There was a nervous joke about what it was that had made this nigger lose his head.

I wondered then if it was real. But now I know that it was.

Headlines tomorrow:

MOTORCYCLISTS FOUND SHOT AT MISS REST STOP
Subhead:
BOOTH IN COSMIC SHIT, UP TO HIS LIPS

—ɷ—

10:45 AM on this surreal day in the life, and Booth washing his face in the kitchen sink. Andries into his bedroom with the shopping bag, heavy with cash and pistols.

Look at the kitchen clock. Only 10:47 in the morning, and several dead to report. With a searing pulse of misery, still see that converted look of innocence on Redbone's feral face just before the .45 went off and then his terrible fall. But I can smell this Joy dish soap and see that flowered dish towel hanging neatly right there.

This is where, in the books and movies, the protagonist calmly or frantically weighs his options. Kill Andries? Yeah, right. Run away? Andries would hear the car. Hoof it? See me making it rapidly down Burdette Street under the sun, clutching my bloody guitar and a bag of underwear, Andries' car backing out of the driveway before I got 100 yards, enraged wildebeest head swiveling to get a bead on me. Call in confederates? Like who, for instance?

Booth decides instead to take a nap. Unfortunately, tiny curled fragments of dream insinuated themselves in a rapid succession. Insanely, a stanza materialized...

*A glimpse of oncoming dream*
*But no way to stop it*
*Or dodge it*

*Or make it*
*Slow down*

At some point, hearing the back door, Booth rouses, peeks out through the blinds. Andries has a laundry basket chock full, into the washroom back of the garage. Comes out presently, drops the empty basket at the back steps. In a few seconds Booth hears the GTO's engine fire up in the driveway. Sleep pulls him back down.

—⬚—

Booth wakes up to a gentle tapping at his door. Jill. Her smile is the same as always. Asks how his writing is going. "Any progress on that new poetry collection you talked about?" Booth stares at her. Dumbly.

"Wesley? Are you ok?" Her brows lowering a bit.

"Uh, yeah." Shaking his head. "Sorry, I just woke up." But that's my voice there, out loud in this dream. Get it on tape, evidence that I exist. In this dream, at least. Try another sentence. "What time is it?"

She looks into the kitchen. "Quarter to twelve."

Only an hour gone by. I thought it had been a month. "Where's Cole?"

"I thought maybe you'd know. The car's not here." Looking down a little. "Ooh, what happened there?" Booth looks down, sees his tee shirt with blood spots. And now his wrist taken by Jill. "Goodness, what bit you there?"

"Oh," glancing furtively over at the guitar. "It was a bramble, some kind of briar. Vicious. I was pulling up some weeds by the garage..."

"You were pulling up weeds?" Dubiously.

"Well, you know. Fire hazard, that sort of thing." Spin a small web of fibs. OK, lies then, but tiny white ones.

"Okaaaay... Well, I'm just here for a sec. I'm meeting a couple of people from school. We're putting together a study group. For a colloquium. I'm gonna hop in the shower." Looks again at Booth's wrist. "Hang on a minute." She goes in the bathroom, returns with a bottle of hydrogen peroxide, some gauze and white tape. "Here, better clean that wrist up." Pauses as Booth looks stupidly at the first-aid supplies.

"Want some help?"

"Oh no. No, I'm ok."

After Jill left, Booth wandered. His mind, and the rest of him too. He wandered outside, looked up at the sky. And down at the grass. See these feet standing here on the grass. Wanders back inside. Rolls a sheet of paper into the black typewriter. Starts typing:

> *It's no field of daisies*
> *This walk up those stairs*
> *That man with his hood*
> *Waiting up there*
>
> *I can see those assembled*
> *Exchange their quick glances*
> *As the band dies down*
> *And the snickers fade out*

*They all know what's coming*
*They've gathered to see*
*A neck yanked at noon*
*And this time it's me*

Booth turns on the radio. Jethro Tull on about *Cross-Eyed Mary*, with her penchant for old lechers and a tooth for freebie gruel. A demented ode to geriatric love on the fringe of a bog near Hampstead. Booth turns up the volume.

Now a news bulletin...

*...WWL-radio has learned that Clarence Gagnard, the late assistant curator at the New Orleans Museum of Art, had in fact been a target of a federal investigation into the April theft of over $600,000 worth of fine art from the museum. Gagnard was found shot to death this morning in his uptown home. The police and federal authorities are investigating, but have no suspects at this time...*

Booth stands up at the termination of this blurb, and marches straight into Jill and Andries' bedroom. Opens that drawer full of underwear and money. Reaches in with timorous grasping hand...

*Bing Bong!* Doorbell like a rifle shot. Money dropped in trembling haste, panties quickly arranged to cover, the drawer pushed shut in shame and fear. For my life's sake I hope it's not Andries, saying he's forgotten his key or some other fatal thing. Through the adjoining bathroom, to his bedroom, Booth doing the chicken walk of criminal stealth. His eyes bugging, teeth bared in a Woody Woodpecker grin of mortal fright.

Next to his table, innocence regained, gathering his wits and a deep breath. Reassemble my bearing to answer the door. But peek down the hallway first as a precaution. And feel my testicles retract. There's a policeman with his hat out there through the sheer curtains and glass. Booth yanks his head back. Now hear knocking. The crystal doorknob turning back and forth.

Presently, the policeman steps away toward the driveway. Booth creeps into the kitchen like an Indian scout. Bespectacled Comanche eyes peeking through the curtain. The cop stops at Booth's Rambler. Cups his face against a side window to see inside. Stands up, looks briefly into the back yard, wanders back up the driveway. After a moment, the cruiser starts and drives off.

As soon as the cop left, Booth started throwing things into pillow cases, scavenging madly and I have to wonder if that is my ordained purpose in this life. I believe some people have thought that, even if they haven't been so bold as to actually say it. Some, in fact, have been so bold. The Remington Rand, the loafers, the guitar, the Twin Reverb. Two trips, then three. Throw everything into the car. A ream of paper burst on impact, a sterile avalanche of bleached paper slithering over everything. Sweat soaking his tee shirt, flooding his glasses.

Now Lenna's things. Booth jerks a sheet off the bed, spreads it out on the floor, dumps every drawer in the bureau onto it, then scrapes the top surface onto it. Armfuls of clothes from the closet, hangers and all. Ties the four corners of the sheet together. Knot comes apart, girl things spill out. The glass stopper pops out of a vial of perfume, releasing clouds of romantic French vapor. Grabs up all the spills, then yanks a cord off the venetian blinds. Blinds come crashing down. Gathers up the four corners again, wraps the cord around the corners, ties it with a plea that the knot was the same as he half-remembered from a some manual or other, some time or other. He looks around the room. Oops, Jeremiah the bullfrog there in the corner. Grabs the frog by its tongue, hauls it all out, throws it into the trunk.

Then, in an orgy of what does it matter now, not to mention no gas money, back into Jill and Andries' bedroom, averting his eyes from their photographs. Into the lingerie drawer. Actually using his pen to excavate through the panties, unable to touch them because of thoughts of Jill and her certain innocence. Grabs a couple of money stacks, leave the rest with the thought that it would be a lesser sin. Arranges things neatly again, and quickly back to his room. Looking around with desperate eyes. Snatches a final box of paper clips and the typewriter eraser off the desk and out to the car.

Sitting in the driver's seat, Booth twists the key. Suddenly, the flash of a thrilling, terrifying thought. His eyes stare blinking over the wheel. Turns the engine back off. Like a crazed moth to a welding arc, he heads for the laundry room back of the garage.

Now in this rotting quarter, doubtful floor of creaking boards, cramped with washing machine, old paint cans, pruning shears, empty flower pots, dusty Shell motor oil cans, a deflated football, a rusted Stilson wrench and a less-rusty pair of Vise-Grips. A short rake with a degraded work glove, fingers shaped whimsically into a peace sign, hailing cheerfully from the tip of the broken haft.

A large wicker laundry hamper there. Booth's eyes move past it, then back themselves up. He gingerly lifts the padded lid, peeks inside. Old clothes, musty and dank with mildew. He grabs the rake, uses the handle minus the glove, digs through the hamper. Finds the rolled top of a paper bag, pulls it quickly out. The bag, due to moisture or fate, bursts silently just as it clears the edge of the hamper, and dumps rolls of money and a revolver clunking and thumping onto the floor. Some of the cash falls back into and around the hamper. A rubber band breaks and one roll explodes in a Las Vegas fantasy of ill-gotten gain. In the middle of the ragged fan of cash, a sober, electric detail: ".357 Magnum" stamped into the barrel of the black revolver.

Booth stands straight up, stunned by the sense that there is a two-faced mirror sprouting up like an obelisk out of the scattering of cash on the dusty floor in this musty room. What came before on one side, what comes after on the other. I believe they call this a crossroads, or an epiphany.

A distant siren goads him back into action. Amongst the old laundry, he finds a faded, mildewed garment with winged pixies dancing. An apron. Spreads it on the floor, scrapes up cylinders of money and loose currency onto the apron, along with the revolver. Spies more of the money behind the hamper, reaches for it, but recoils when a cockroach runs up his arm. Ties a half-assed knot to hold the chunky apron together, then another. Siren closer now. Booth stepping with the stealth of terror back to the driveway, notes of legal tender dripping and fluttering onto the overgrown concrete stepping stones. He peeks around the corner of the house, sees a roaring fire engine wail past.

Into the car, apron in the back seat, along with the rest of his life. Turns the key. Heart stops as the starter sticks for a half-second, then grunts alive. Backs the car out, neck twisting crazily, looking for Andries or the police. Or maybe even God, wagging a playful finger at this clear breach of scripture, stealing and so forth.

Finally, Booth away up the narrow street, a crazy imperiled desperado in his little gray smoking bronco.

—m—

Booth dials Lenna's work number at Tulane from a pay phone on St. Charles. A woman answers. "Records."

"Can I speak to Lenna please?"

"One moment please."

A delay of hair-raising duration, then, "This is Lenna Steadman."

"Lenna. Can you please get out of there and meet me somewhere?"

"Whatever's the matter, Wesley?"

"A very large problem. Can you get out of there?"

"Can't it wait until 4 o'clock?"

"Nope, better not. Serious shit." Booths looks around. "This going to sound paranoid, but just start walking, um, back toward St. Charles. I'll find you." Starts to hang up, then "Wait, wait! What are you wearing?"

—m—

"What do you mean? *How* did he kill them? Why did he *do* that?" Lenna's eyes wide, brows popped up in shock.

"He fucking shot them. It was some busted art deal." Booth lights a cigarette with shaking fingers.

"Art...?"

"Yeah. Long story. He says they were gonna kill him. Us, actually, since I was there too. And that's pretty much what it looked like to me, I guess." Booth looks around, scanning the street for Andries' car.

"You have to go to the police, Wesley. Straight away."

"I don't think I'd better do that. I hit one of them in the head with the guitar."

"Your guitar? Why?"

"Yeah. Oh man, *I don't fucking believe this.* I got to get out of here." Booth steers through the roiling stew of Audubon Boulevard, the sun a fatal dripping blare of light.

Lenna crosses her legs and lays a hand on his arm. "Wesley, you've got to calm down now." She looks at him for a moment. "Is it possible you may have exaggerated some of this?"

"Hey, I know this all sounds made up, but how well do you really know Cole?"

"Just through Jill. I first met him at the party in Alexandria."

"Did Jill tell you he was the guy in that story the bike guy was telling? The one that cut that dude's ears off?" Booth drags deeply on the Winston. "And have I mentioned that the guy telling that story was the first one he blew away? Just like *POW*, and then the shit was in the fan."

"Bloody hell." Lenna takes a breath, her eyes blinking.

She sits silently for a moment, then, "Why did you hit the one? Was he shooting?"

"No...there was a fight...it looked like he was getting the best of Andries. I don't know, man. It just seemed like I had to do it. Andries said one of them pulled a gun on him, but that's not the way I saw it."

"Christ, Wesley. What's your plan?"

"I'm leaving. Right now. You have to come with me."

"Wesley, that's just daft. I can't leave now. I can't leave at all. I've got a job." She looked sideways. "And you can't leave either. You've got to tell the police."

"Listen, there's something else." Pauses. A confession coerced by circumstance. "*Shit*. Ok, I ripped off a bunch of money from Andries."

"Why in God's name did you do that?"

"I freaked. But for a good reason."

"What good reason?"

"He thinks I'll talk. And fuck, now I've put you in this shit too. *Fuck!*"

"Won't the police protect you?"

"A cop showed up at the house today. Didn't look like he was there to protect anybody." Booth makes a left turn onto Claiborne.

"And that's not the end of it, baby. I'm pretty sure Cole killed another guy. I heard something on the radio about this guy from the museum that got shot last night. It sounds like he was mixed up in the art scheme too."

"How do you know that?"

"I don't know it. But I'd bet on it. Remember when Cole left last night?"

She pauses. "How much money did you take, anyway?"

"I don't even know. It's in that apron back there."

"Apron?"

Lenna turns around, hauls the grimy garment onto her polyester lap and unties a knot. "Dear Christ." The revolver tumbles out, thunk on the tatty nap of the floorboard carpet. Lenna looks at Booth with eyes popped wide.

Booth looks back at her, tensely. "Your stuff is already in the trunk."

Lenna looks back down at the apron, then raises her big round eyes. She asks this pivotal question:

"Did you bring Jeremiah?"

And now the humpty gray Rambler rolling free across the Bonnet Carré Spillway on Interstate 10, just west of Kenner. Westward ho, laden with felonies, engorged with hope. Fat, felonious hope.

Booth lays out the whole story for Lenna. At the telling of the actual shootings, Lenna closed her eyes. "What an awful thing, Wesley." She shook out a cigarette, snapped off the white filter.

"Does Jill know you've left?"

"Baby, I didn't say a word to anybody except you. I thought about Jill, of course, as one would, but what could I do? I doubt she'd believe me if I told her. You almost didn't believe me, and she's like married to him. I'm sure she doesn't have a clue. I mean, I know she's hip that he deals pot, but that's probably all. And I admit I sorta panicked. Snagged the money and just split. Wish I hadn't, I guess, but if I hadn't, I'd be on foot. I didn't even have gas money."

As if in consonance, the Rambler bucked slightly and backfired as Booth took his foot off the gas to accommodate a slow moving truck.

Like a jolt from Jupiter, Lenna asks this question: "What about Howard?"

Booth looks at her quickly. "What?"

"Jill told me the story, Wesley."

—◆◆◆—

Booth and Lenna sitting at the lunch counter of the Bobcat Diner in La Place. Raining a bit outside, and can we ever just get clear of this spongy, saturated habitat? I want to see cacti, saguaros, road runners and coyotes. Sand. Tumbleweeds. Cowpokes on cayuses...

"I don't care, Wesley. You have got to do it." Lenna broke the filter off another L&M, lit it with Booth's Zippo. "You can't just leave the state without letting your mum know. With your brother and all, you just can't."

Lenna looks Booth in the face.

"Wesley?"

Booth blows out a defeated breath. "God damn it." Holds out his hand. "Got any change?"

—◆◆◆—

Mrs. Booth answers the phone. "*Wesley, where in God's name are you? I left word for you just ages ago.*"

"I'm in La Place, Mom. Just wanted to touch bases with you before heading west. We've got some big doings coming up out in Reno, and I've got to get out there pronto."

"What are you talking about?"

"Reno, Nevada. I've finally got a serious in with the music scene out there..."

"*Will you hush and listen to me please!*"

"Mom, I hate to be in a hurry, but I've only got a minute here." Booth looking toward the highway for the black GTO.

"This'll take less than a minute, then. You have to go and pick up Howard."

"Pick up Howard? Mom, Pineville is hundreds of miles from here."

"Well, good news for you. He's not in Pineville. He's in New Iberia..."

"New Iberia? What the f...? What's he doing there?"

"He's at a special facility down there, and he needs to get out of there. I'm sure you've heard about the storm coming in. Oh, they told me Howard needs some supplies, too..."

"Storm?" Booth stares at the phone. A gust of wind blows up his hair, rattles the armor-clad cord against the glass.

"Wait a second. Did you say you left word about something?"

"Your friend Jill's mother goes to church with Fran. I just got lucky this time and got your phone number. I was starting to believe I'd never hear from you again. Write this down..."

*ten*

# *red devil*

In that thin, dismal annulus between the fungal loam of Lousiana and the roiling grey sky, Booth's face straining forward over the Rambler's steering wheel. A cloud of spray steaming off its wheels.

And Lenna there, rolling a joint on a copy of People magazine, flakes of dope speckling the face of a star.

"Uh, would you please hand me a beer, luv?" He lit a Winston. "When you're finished with that, of course. Listen, if we get pulled over, you better hide that shit. I've got enough going on without that."

"You're worrying far too much, Wesley. Just try to relax. We're going to be fine. Nobody cares about pot anymore." She completed her craft, licked the joint with a gesture that Booth would have found both demure and provocative under another circumstance.

A tinny voice on the radio broke in, disrupting "*Sugar Sugar*," by the Archies:

*The National Weather Service has issued a hurricane watch effective 6 PM today for the coastal areas of Texas and Louisiana. Hurricane Edith has veered from her path toward Texas to a more north-easterly course. Hurricane hunter aircraft dispatched from the National Hurricane Center in Miami have measured winds near the eye of the storm in excess of 110 MPH. As of 2 PM, the eye of Edith was located at approximately 28 degrees North, 94 degrees West, about 100 miles south-southeast of the mouth of the Sabine River. The powerful storm now appears to be heading north-northeast at about 15 miles an hour. In addition to high winds, torrential rains and high tides should be expected as Edith approaches the coast. The Coast Guard has issued a small craft advisory for the coast of Louisiana from the mouth of the Sabine River to the Mississippi delta. Residents of low-lying areas in the watch zone should immediately move to higher ground. Refugee shelters have been set up by the Red Cross. Stay tuned to your local station for shelter locations and important storm information...*

Concurrent with the burst of static that terminated this announcement, a blast of crosswind makes the car stagger, the hood tugging at the rusted coat hanger that holds it shut. A seizure of anxiety, wrestling with the steering wheel, eyes watching the roadside trees for signs of riotous winds. Booth quaffs the beer recklessly. Lenna offers him the joint under scudding clouds of doom.

He gives her a sideways look. "Thanks, but no. Can you see I've got a situation here to deal with?" He took his foot off the gas and the Rambler made a pipsqueak backfire. An ambulance passed by, siren yowling. "See? Fuck!" Booth's eyes wide and white.

"No need to be shitty about it, luv. I'm no expert, but that hurricane they're on about is a day or so out, isn't it?"

"Yeah, well let me give you a clue. What I'm concerned about are the peripheral effects. You probably wouldn't know about this, but these things can throw off tornadoes before they ever hit land. Just give me a little slack here, OK?"

Lenna's lips tighten, then she returns to her magazine, leaving a whistling silence in which the car is bullied by gusts and the gray rake of rain. The single wiper blade worked feebly against the torrent.

New Iberia, Louisiana. Of all possible destinations in anticipation of a hurricane. A cosmic joke coming into focus here, punctuated by a rustle in the ether, a sardonic snickering of the gods. All I need to complete the picture is a neon-pink lightning rod on this chalky, faded roof and a chain dangling underneath. As if to emphasize the fever of his thoughts, a sheet of lightning flared arrogantly just to the east, white as a pillowcase at Holiday Inn.

*"John the fucking Baptist."*

Booth crushed his empty can. A pause to garner some good will, patience and a smile.

"Lenna, luv, would you please hand me another beer?"

She twists around, makes a styrofoam squeak and slush of ice. Returns with a 16 ounce Schlitz, fat, cold and resonant.

Booth steers the shaking, pinging, overheating Rambler into a white shell parking lot, much like any other this close to the Gulf. The rain, teasingly, had tapered off to nothing. A smell of marine life on the breeze as he gets out of the car, and a Springer spaniel stares aggressively from the back seat of a '65 Ford parked next to him. Jesus, even the creatures have got my number. Booth shoves his face down to the glass, eyes wide and teeth glaring. This produces a storm of woofing, the dog a wedge of belligerence and spraying of spittle.

"For God's sake, Wesley. Leave it alone, can't you?"

"Me? The thing *went* for me. What do you expect me to do, lose my arm gracefully?"

Booth looks around. Store fronts battened and people battening. A traffic light swaying slightly, flashing red for danger.

Surely there's another place for me, perhaps at 8000 feet, amongst the snow and the aspen. I know it can't be true, but I think some of this may be my mother's fault. She has an in with Our Father Who Art In Heaven, and she's calling in her chits. I mean, really, how else could this situation be explained? Right on the cusp of escape, and now this business. Feel a filament or tendril wrapping around my leg.

Lenna holds the bag containing the Ex-Lax and mineral oil aloft. "Do you want to bring these in straight away, or come back and get them?"

Booth stares at her, a dangerous pulse beating in his neck. "Just leave the shit in the car. If they want them, we'll send someone out for them. I'm sure they have menials here."

Standing here at the desk inside the trailer. A young woman typing madly. An older one on the phone, with a worried face. It beats me that these people are bewildered when death clouds pay them a visit. As though it's uncommon to have a storm knocking on the windows here on the Gulf coast. The woman glancing up. "I'll be right with you, sir."

"Oh, just take your time, by all means. We'll be over here looking at your prints of the last hurricane."

Lenna, seeking to distract, points out a portrait of a pelican on the paneled wall. Booth responds that it was probably blown inland during Audrey, in 1957. "They found it hanging in the rigging of a derelict shrimp boat. That picture was taken just before it died. It was a casualty."

Finally, the girl at the desk hangs up the phone. "Can I help you folks?"

"Have you got any morphine? An IV drip would be the bees knees right about now..."

Lenna interrupts. "We've come to transport Howard Booth. Is he ready?"

Walking down this paneled hall, I notice that the decor reeks of gloom, even with Lenna by my side. The hallway carpet is thin, the door is green, and there's that aroma of piss again. The nurse knocks gently. Opens the door, and there is Howard. His tongue protrudes slightly, as though concentrating. He sees Lenna and his eyes open with something like interest.

The nurse says, "We've had a couple of little issues with Howard's attention to the female staff." She raised her eyebrows at Lenna, a fusion of seriousness and girlish conspiracy. "Why don't ya'll have a seat and we'll get his papers ready. It'll be a few minutes. We've got three other patients leaving because of the storm. You know the sheriff ordered us to evacuate because of the trailers." She made off down the hall, leaving the door open.

"Trailers. *Did you hear that?* Can you imagine anyone pulling *trailers* up in this unspeakable, fucking, hurricane-bait town for *patients* to live in?" Booth stalking the room like a stork captured from the neighboring estuary.

"Wesley, please calm down. We'll be out of here in just a bit, won't we?"

"Fuck. Where'd she go anyway? To get a goddamned net?"

"They'll be dropping a net over you if you don't take a grip on yourself." Howard had started humming his tune, rocking back and forth. Lenna sits down and places her hand on his shoulder. "Poor thing. Really, Wesley, you're upsetting him."

Booth jerks a cord, opening the venetian blinds. Outside the rain was coming down with fresh vigor, and he could see a patrol car parked in the lot, lights rotating. A deputy in a yellow slicker got in and there was a loud squawk of radio. Wind slaps the trailer and rattles the rusted crank-out window. Booth snaps the blinds closed. "I wonder if we could just get moving here..."

The nurse comes back in with a Glad bag full of medicine.

"Here are Howard's medications. You'll have to sign for them, and we have a few more papers that have to be filled out." Booth accepts the bag. Orange bottles of psychotropics with their labels. *Take with food...Do not operate machinery while taking this medication...Alcohol may intensify the effect...Do not take this medication if pregnant or nursing.* How about if you're a hunchback? Or a Catholic? I think they've left out a few things. Haven't covered all the bases. Maybe I should have a few of each, just to see...

The nurse watches Booth jiggling the bag. "We need to get to the paperwork pretty quick, too. The sheriff just told us we have to get out of here in less than an hour. He said the highway back up to Lafayette's starting to flood." Opens the door, turns back. "Oh, Howard had a nice big bowel movement just while ago, so you should be good there."

Booth rubs an insane itch in his nose, then turns to Lenna. An intonation of lightness to stop the rising bile of horror in his gullet.

"Uh, luv, would you mind filling out those papers? I've got this ocular migraine that's making it hard to read the fine print."

Lenna gave him a look, then turned to the nurse. "Will that conform to the protocol?" That English breath of upper crust.

The nurse said "Sure. We just have to have the responsible family member sign the release form and a couple of things."

"Responsible? Well, that would be Wesley, then, I'm sure."

Booth stared at the back of her retreating head.

When they left the room, Booth once again looked out the window. A gust shouldered the trailer with a bump, inadequate frame creaking under its film of tin.

As they placed Howard—immunized against the weather—into the back seat, the rain started again, this time blown by a reckless wind. "You all be careful now." The nurse hurrying across the shells, her skirt molded wetly to her legs, showing her girdle, hand on Nightingale cap.

Booth and Lenna into the car, sitting on the blankets Lenna had folded up over the springs of the front seat. Booth turns the key. And hear that impotent grind. Once again. And then, just a click. "Fuck."

"Won't it start?"

"Fucking thing. God damned piece of shit."

"Christ, Wesley. We should get out of here. Can you ever fix it?"

Now Booth underneath the car, legs sticking out from under the driver's door. Water streaming in drips from the grease of the frame and rust of exhaust pipes. His hand snaking up with the revolver—the only tool he could find—to bang the starter.

"*Turn the key.*" He rapped obscurely at the machinery in the intermittent but undeniably increasing wind. Nothing. "*Try it again.*"

He hears a slight click. Encouraged, Booth smacks harder at the thing. "*Turn the key again.*" Nothing. No more clicks. Enraged, he swings the pistol randomly within its limited arc, grazing the shells and the undercarriage in unavailing fury. The handle breaks into its constituent walnut halves, leaving a screw rattling in the grip frame. A blue and white triangle of barked skin on the knuckle of his thumb, and bright drop of blood, instantly diluted by raindrip.

"*Son of a fucking bitch.*" He wriggled out from under on his shoulder blades, gun on his belly. "Miserable waste of ..." Encounters somebody's legs. Looks up.

As certainly as Jesus on a crutch, there's Andries' prehistoric face up there, looking down. Rain streaming over his shoulders, a hand reaching down to help Booth up.

—◆◆◆—

"What's wrong up underneath there, Booth?" Andries' mouth gave a smile, but the eyes poked into Booth with mordant interest. Booth relinquishes the pistol to Andries' beckoning hand.

"Missed you when you left, man. Wanted to say goodbye, you know?" Blood roaring and squealing in Booth's ears.

"I think maybe you accidentally took something that didn't belong to you when you left. Anything ringing a bell?" Andries bends to look into the car. See Lenna's ashen face looking straight at Booth, Howard in the back, nodding to his left.

Booth hears his tremulous voice. "Hey Cole. Wow. Great to see you, man. We..."

"Come on, Booth. You gonna try to bullshit me some more?" That sardonic look. "Mr. combat vet? Mr. Purple Heart? My ass."

"Look, Cole, I know this looks bad, but..."

Andries spreads his hands, amiably. "Hey, there's no problem here, Booth. People make mistakes. I just want what's mine, that's all. Just give it up nice and quiet, and you and Spot can head off into the desert. Or where the fuck ever. I'll even give you some gas money." He bends again, looking into the back seat. "And Howard too. Howard, right?" Booth nods dumbly.

"Damn, Booth, dude looks just like you...after you shit yourself blind." Andries raises a peace sign and a smile to Howard, the way one would to a child. A pepper of rain, borne by a gust, spattered them.

Andries tapped the Rambler's fender with the muzzle of the revolver. "Ok, this thing's dead, right?"

The trailer door squawks open, blows back against the trailer with a bang. The two nurses come out, wrestle the door shut and lock it. "Ya'll still here, *cher*?"

Andries, pistol casually behind his back, says, "Problem with the old jalopy here, but don't worry, I've got mine."

The older nurse says, "Deputy just called again. He said something about the highway, but the phone went dead. I expect y'all better get a move on. Get back up to Lafayette."

"Thanks. Y'all ladies be careful, now, hear?" Andries affecting the accent of the South, somewhat sardonically. Watching the women get into an Oldsmobile. Smiles again as they drive off.

"Ok, Spot, get out and go stand by your man. No, better stand over on this side of the car." Motions with the pistol toward Howard. "Booth, is this guy really out of it? Tell me the truth now, I don't want any surprises." Booth nods.

Andries reaches in for the keys. Goes around and opens the trunk, starts pulling clothes out, drops them into the wet shells. Perfume bottles, costume jewelry, knicks and knacks scattered callously. Jeremiah the bullfrog briefly airborne, then listing leftward in a puddle, sponging up muddy water.

Booth looks at Lenna on the opposite side of the Rambler. She waits until Andries has his head in the trunk, then mimes a gun, pointing it at herself and then Booth, then Howard. As if Booth didn't already realize it, her implication was clear. They weren't getting out of this thing alive.

Andries comes to the back door, opens it, tumbles the Twin Reverb violently onto the ground with a fatal crunch of glass vacuum tubes and splintered plywood. Pokes into the back of the amp. Now the Les Paul, dumped out of its case, booted cruelly across the shells with a dying twang and snap of strings.

Andries directs a venomous stare at Booth, then at Lenna. "I better find what I'm looking for real fucking quick, Booth. Understand me?"

"It's not in the car, Cole."

"No? So where is it, then?"

"In Lafayette. Bus station locker."

Andries pauses, straightens up. "So you got wind I was coming?"

"No. When I realized I fucked up, I knew you'd be pretty pissed. The plan was to get out of the state, then let you know where to find it."

"So you were going to be generous? With my money?"

"No, not really. Self preservation."

"Come on, Booth. You know I'm a reasonable guy." He looked from Booth to Lenna, then back. "Ok, pitch me the key."

"The key's not here either."

Andries' eyebrows come together. "Come again?"

"We left it in the hotel room. Lafayette."

"And why's that?"

Lenna interjects: "I put it in my makeup kit. And I didn't see the sense in bringing makeup out in the rain."

"Uh huh." Pauses. A slap of wind and rain intervened. "Ok, everybody in my car, and let's get up the road. Come on. The broad and that one"...he waggled the pistol in Howard's direction..."in the back. Booth, you in front. Let's go!"

—◆—

Twenty miles to Lafayette, the four of them packed into Andries' black GTO. Booth in the passenger seat, Lenna behind him. Howard behind Andries. Muscled by gusts and torrents.

Another storm warning on the radio.

*...Hurricane Edith is now expected to make landfall on the Louisiana coast sometime before midnight tonight. All but essential personnel have been evacuated from dozens of Gulf drilling platforms in the storm's path. Residents should already have evacuated areas near the coast...*

Less than a quarter-mile mile out of town, a barricade and a yellow warning light, tipped over and flashing through the muddy water. A wind riffed lake beyond in the dismal gray gloaming. Andries comes to a stop, spits a maternal expletive at the dash.

"Jesus God." Lenna's hand on Booth's shoulder.

On the west side of the highway, a motel, closed for the storm or maybe forever. Six cottages, 1950s-style, pink shingles, set up on pilings, lit up by the Pontiac's headlights. Arranged in a concave arc facing the highway. Shut down and black. Andries turns around, pulls up in front of the accommodation.

After unsuccessfully trying another one, Andries breaks into one of the middle cottages, using something from his pocket with criminal talent. Herds them inside. See boxes of toilet paper, painting supplies, cleaning supplies, stacked and unstacked.

Some scrounging by Andries with his flashlight turned up two candle stubs and an empty coal oil lamp. He fills the lamp from a can of linseed oil, and soon a dreadful coziness filled the room. A nightmare of floral wallpaper all around, ancient television bolted to the wall, smell of mildew. A stunning crack of thunder shook the room.

Booth in a state of panic, ears stuffed shut with fingers. Andries' face a derisive mask, his voice taunting:

"Now what you gonna do, Booth? That's a bad ass storm out there. I thought I heard something about a tornado while ago." A quiet chuckle. "You dig tornadoes, Booth?"

"Why don't you just leave him alone?" Lenna's assertive plea.

See Andries turn slowly toward Lenna. Takes a swig from a half-pint of whiskey.

Quietly. "You his mama, now...Spot?" Eyes glittering in the flutter of the lamp, a grim smile tightly on his lips. Lenna shrinking against the wall, her eyes wide.

Booth's unavailing voice, a trembling whisper in the face of this domination. "Come on, Cole, she..."

Andries turning back. Booth can see the square handle of the Colt stuck in his belt. Just reach out and grab it, a quick, final act and freedom. Save this day and all the rest. Any small blunder or hesitation, though, and wind up convulsing, bleeding from the mouth and the eyes. A gust of wind shrieked suddenly under the door.

Look up with anguished eyes to see Andries' frank smile of contempt. "Thinkin' about something, Booth?" He snorted gently. "Nah, I didn't think so." He pulled out his flat bottle of whiskey again, unscrewed the cap and threw back his head, the bottle straight up. See the beard under his neck, think of a quick razor slice, the carotid emptying itself in three-foot spurts as Andries tried wildly to pinch off the flow, dancing the *danse macabre*. If I had a razor. Andries screwed the cap back on the brown bottle. Holds it up to check the contents.

Now a forthright look. "Hey, how 'bout a little drink of whiskey, Booth?" Holds out the half-pint with an inch left in the bottom.

"Here you go, man." He flicked the bottle quickly past Booth's reaching hand. A wet crash and Booth turning dumbly to look, brown hash of shards glinting dully on the bathroom tiles.

"Oops. Damn, I'm sorry, Booth. Better watch your step in there." Laughs roughly. He cocked his head. "Woo, listen to that wind out there. Spooky, man." Laughing again. He turned back toward Lenna.

It's 7:15 PM, going dark. Oh that wind in the oak trees through the thin, rattling window. Howard hums his tune.

At exactly 8 o'clock, Andries says, companionably, "Booth,

you reckon you can get him to shut that shit up? It's starting to annoy me."

Booth clears his throat. "It's not something I can do anything about." Lenna's eyes come up quickly. Andries' narrow.

"Well, maybe I can help, then. Hold this light, Spot." Stands up quickly, takes a step, grabs Howard by the shoulders, screams in his face. "*Shut the fuck up!*" Howard goes silent, raises up a ghastly face of friendship toward Andries.

Booth hears his own voice rise up in a hideous, primal wail and is astounded to see his hand clutching the bail of a gallon can of Glidden Semi-Gloss Interior White, swinging it directly at Andries' head.

Andries turned with an unbelieving expression, reaching for the gun as he tried to duck away in slow motion. The paint can nevertheless hit Andries' primitive head and Booth was shocked to see him go down. Lenna shrieked a warning. "*Look out, look out!*" Andries came up off the floor, the .45 just clearing his belt as Booth flung the can at his head. Impossibly, Booth saw the bottom edge of the can connect with Andries' caveman forehead right at the hairline and the skin split pinkly. As Andries went backward, *POW*, the concussive wave of gunblast, lantern exploding, ears stunned and ringing in the dark. Booth dove without hesitation or option into the blackness where Andries was, a terrifying and unavoidable commitment.

An arm of steel was instantly around his neck, smell of sweat and grunting breath, Booth's hands slipping desperately up Andries' left arm toward the gun. He felt his neck being bent forward with the express intent of breaking or strangling. Spasmodically, responding to years of movie conditioning, Booth drove an elbow rearward toward Andries' stomach. A slippery miss and his neck bent even further. His right thumb touched something he recognized as the hammer of the .45. An advantage. Andries was stronger, but Booth's arms were longer. He stretched to grasp the gun hand, surprised that Andries didn't seem able to escape or prevail. Surprise gave way to a dangerous feeling of pressure in his head that threatened to pop out his eyes. Realizing that his left hand was free, he suddenly had a solution.

With a slight feeling of impropriety, and also one of pure desperation, he jammed his hand into Andries' jeans and took him by the genitals. He was immediately stunned when, instead of release, he found his head tucked over to an impossible angle and his forehead being ground into the degraded linoleum floor. He could feel two things. The shame of failure despite his grip on another man's balls, and the sliding into defeat as the strength of his right hand faded away. Now his grasping left hand was yanked out of the other's pants and Andries' voice rasping in his ear.

"Woo, *shit*, Booth, I thought you had me there. By the balls, huh? *By the balls?*" Booth's head bouncing off the floor, repeatedly, his left eye full of some liquid, Lenna's British voice pleading in the ebbing background.

Booth came around to find himself face down on linoleum in the half dark. There was a voice speaking softly and unintelligibly, but with menacing tone. My life here at the end of this fraying rope. Abandon hope, all ye without a magnum.

And yet, surprising how closely nothing to lose can resemble hope.

With astonishing clarity, given the dim flicker of candle stub, one eye full of lifeblood, and his glasses who knew where, Booth could see stacked cans of paint, labeled with various faded and dripped-over brands. Under the edge of the bed, amongst this and that, a small can of something, likely associated with painting or some other laborious pastime. Booth reaches slowly out, hoping Andries was distracted by his current depredation. By tiny metric fractions, Booth brings the can closer. Red Devil Lye says the label. Estimate it to be maybe half-full. Outside, the world was coming apart.

With the smallest possible movements, Booth maneuvers his left hand into place. Tries the cap. Lefty loosey. Cap off. Thus heeled, and shockingly callous of his remaining life, he begins a glacially slow roll toward Andries' voice, in minutes of degrees, maybe even seconds. His bad eye completed the roll first, requiring a few more degrees of the head. See Andries sitting on a chair, the can that had recently opened his forehead underneath it. His face jerked slightly in the fluttering campfire dimness of the candles, showing a white pad of toilet paper stuck to the black gash of blood on his head.

Booth remains in this position, waiting for a cosmic balance to tip in his favor. Within minutes, his neck muscles start to cramp and vibrate. He pinches the skin of his left thigh to distract.

After a while, Andries stands up, steps to the sink in the alcove next to the bathroom. Turns on the water, bends down, cups some up onto his face.

Now Andries' face comes up from the sink, streaming water. His eyes pop wide and blinking, the way one does. And in the flickering candlelight mirror, see Booth with left eye bleeding black, standing right behind him with a handful of hellfire.

With no further thought, Booth's hand comes around and smashes the lye into Andries' eyes. Andries' hands come up to his face. Booth's left hand to Andries' belt for the .45. Grabs it as Andries' elbow knocks him back against the wall, falling over boxes. Andries staggers to the door, issuing curses, knocking Howard over. Crashes into the door, opens it. A staggering blast of wind fills the room with spray and debris. Andries stumbles off the porch toward his car, strobe-lit in mid-air by the flash of a lightning bolt. Lenna bangs the door shut.

"*Help me, help me! Wesley!*" The two of them shove the bed and boxes in front of the door. Booth grabs Howard off the bed, steers him away from the front of the room.

The wind suddenly drops, hear the car door slam, grunting, panting, a deluge of curses. Then POW!, a bullet comes wild through the wall above the window. Chunks of plaster and lath falling from the ceiling. Next one under the window, fluffing the mattress cover and blowing up a paint can on the bed. Turpentine stink of oil-based paint, feel it on the neck. Booth aims the .45 at the door, pulls the trigger. Nothing. Pulls back the slide, hear that machined clank as it chambered a fat cartridge.

"Hold your ears." Fires through the center of the door. *BAM!* Again. *BAM!*

And then a *tink* as something from the silence outside hits the window. Now a *ping*, followed by the beginning of an awful booming roar.

Booth herds Lenna and Howard into the bathroom, crunching on the smashed bottle of whiskey, smell the fumes. A crazy, irrelevant, but oddly objective thought. *It really does sound like a train. Chuka chuka chuka...* Hugs Howard tight, Lenna tighter. Waiting, resigned, for Judgment Day.

Now the groaning of boards and the strafing of hail or artifacts against the cottage. An asthmatic feel of pressure drop, Lenna's face trembling tightly against his neck. Eyes riveted to the door in the feeble flicker of the lantern. Howard hums louder.

The din peaks with an appalling sound of destruction, a blown window, and toppling boxes. The candle blows out. Finally the howling demon mouth outside subsides to a heavy but less violent downpour.

Booth and Lenna venture warily out of the bathroom, Booth's Zippo held aloft for light. They bring Howard out, take up a position in the far corner behind these boxes, cover the door in case Andries comes back.

—〰—

Booth awoke with a violent jerk, light in his face, the pistol up and pointing. Eyes blinking desperately, Howard still asleep. Lenna standing with the curtain pulled back from a smashed window, looking out, sunlight streaming in. Booth comes up now to her side, see the mute look of wonder on her face. Looking out at the scene of a war.

Three of the six cabins in the arc were gone. Sun shining bright on the splintered mayhem of shingles and glass. A smell of torn wood, a lightness in the soul, the spring morning feel of childhood in a world laid waste and made perfect. Howard rolled over and farted.

Andries' car lies on its roof in a field of ruination which comprises the roadway, passenger door blown forward as if by a bomb. But where was Andries?

"Stay here, Lenna." He stepped out the door and pasted himself against the wall. See lenticular clouds moving peacefully toward the eastern horizon.

Sidestepping carefully along the wall like a cartoon, Booth suddenly fears that Andries' arm might snake out from underneath the cottage, grab him by the ankles and drag him into hell. Kneels down with the .45 and peeks under the ravaged skirt of pink shingles and tar paper. Nothing but foundation pilings, plumbing, tattered cobwebs and a lawnmower, the rusty nameplate clearly legible on the engine: Briggs and Stratton.

Booth stands up. Presently, about to give up the hunt, he hears a popping sound. Steps around a downed pecan tree and looks up to see a live wire dangling from a tilted creosote power pole next to the road.

Several feet above the ground, King Cole Andries levitates in midair, back against the pole, Neanderthal face blistered, swollen, almost unrecognizable. His shirt and the toilet paper bandage are gone, his torso plastered with debris. A spark popped between the tip of the wire and Andries' blackened left ear with every other swing. After a brief moment of paranormal shock, Booth moves carefully closer, pistol cocked and aimed at the floating apparition.

From the better vantage point, Booth can see the upturned end of a J-shaped galvanized steel footing spike protruding from Andries' sternum, five inches below the collarbones.

The Rambler, once they got back to it, started instantly. It appeared to be undamaged, despite the proximity of the traffic light, which Booth had to drag away from the driver's door in order to open it. Unsurprisingly, the Les Paul was gone, and the Twin Reverb, wedged forcibly under the frame of the mental health trailer, was beyond salvation. The trailer itself was racked into a slightly concave parallelogram with twisted black holes for windows. A cheery yellow curtain flapped sadly behind one of them. Dull yellow fiberglass tufts of insulation stuck out here and there where the tin had ripped.

While they were saving Jeremiah—discovered amongst a collection of flotsam at the edge of a vast but ebbing estuarial puddle—a police car cruised by. The officer stuck a red bullhorn out his window and bellowed, "Y'all ok, buddy?" Despite Booth's appearance—knot on the forehead, blackened eye, blood on his shirt, glasses minus the entire right earpiece, paint in his hair, and the Colt absent-mindedly but plainly stuck in his belt—the cop appeared satisfied by a wave of Booth's hand and drove on. Booth put Jeremiah, wrung into mere squishiness, into the back seat with Howard.

Once they reached an unobstructed stretch of road, Booth pipes up. "Well. I guess that settles the issue of what to do on the first day of our vacation."

Lenna looks sideways at him. "My God." After a bit, she says, "Now what happens, Wesley? What about the police, I mean. Jill?"

"I think we best just get up the road right now. I'm pretty sure nobody can tie us to Andries. Besides, I mean, we didn't actually do anything illegal. Except for the money, I guess, but it was stolen money anyway, like twice or three times removed, wasn't it? Seems to me that all that stuff kind of cancels itself out. But there is Jill, though..."

—ⴜ—

A rest stop just south of Ville Platte, on US 167.

Booth helps Howard into the rudimentary facility, does what he has to do to help. When they get back to the car, Booth finds Lenna bent over a discovery. In her hand reposes a baby bird with black bead eyes, nearly naked, and shivering. "I found this one near the loo. Just over there. It must have been blown down in the storm."

Booth feels a push at his shoulder. Howard insinuates his face closer to the little bird. As Booth and Lenna watch him carefully, he reaches out a trembling finger, gently touches the bird's beak with tiny taps. After a moment, Lenna takes Howard's hand and makes it into a cup. She slowly rolls the little bird into his hand. Howard stops humming, glances from the bird to Lenna's face, then back again.

Booth buys a carton of worms at a bait shop in Ville Platte, after a brief contretemps between Lenna and the bait stand proprietor over the $50 bill Booth got out of the apron in the trunk. Amicably resolved when Booth tells the man to keep the change.

Lenna turns around to where the bird is nestled in toilet paper, in a spare carton generously donated by the *nouveau riche* bait man, in Howard's lap. Howard occasionally touching the little bird with a gentle fingertip. When it opened its beak, Lenna dropped in a worm.

"They seem to be getting on well." She looks back at Booth. "I wonder what kind of bird that is, anyway?"

Booth lights a Winston. Over there, to the east, see the yellow and green grass flattened by the wind, rising up a slight hill to a house. Likely the home of a farmer. Now the explosive wail of a chain saw and a white rooster-tail of chips from a blown-down pine.

I can see lenticular clouds drifting northeast like vague zeppelins. And hear this pinging engine in full smoky surge. Pitted asphalt road in front of me, with unfortunately flattened creatures and black bumps of tar and brown puddles for tadpoles, leading north. Leading west too, where the cactus erupts flowering in spring and tumbleweeds roll in waves like buffalo herds across the salt flats.

Waves and molecules. The tendrils and filaments that hold it all together.

Booth feels Lenna touch his hand, tender from the lye he'd rinsed off last night, on the blanket between them.

"Wesley? The bird?"

"Um." Blinks his eyes. Breathes in a breath, lets it out slowly. "Mockingbird, I think."

*A tiny wave*
*Disturbs the lie*
*Of a gently wafting*
*Thread*

*And twists it*
*And warps it*
*Into a dream*

*A tale*
*Of joy*
*Or dread*

# ACKNOWLEDGMENTS

My greatest debt of gratitude is to my good sister, Victoria Jones Witty, who always supported me, even when I was least supportable.

Had it not been for the mentoring and gentle exhortations of my friend James N. Frey, Booth would likely have died on my hard drive.

My wonderful daughter, Corianne Jessica Jones-Mataban. Thanks for being my kid, and congratulations on surviving my fumbling attempts at parenthood. You make it all worthwhile.

My brother, Matthew Stanton Jones, who thought I was the best guitarist ever. Gone too soon…

My mother, Routh K. Jones, who, despite being widowed with three kids in the middle of Louisiana, no job, and no insurance money, somehow managed to keep a roof over our heads. She also kept her sense of humor, her courage, and her burning, shameless, even embarrassing, love for every form of beauty. She lived nearly the whole of her life in Louisiana, but a big chunk of her heart belonged to the mountains of the American West. She showed them to us on one crazy, 10-day, impossibly cheap trip in a 1963 Rambler station wagon. My own heart has been there ever since. Thanks, Mama!

My father, Arthur Leroy Jones. Roy. He died when I was but 11. To be honest, I knew him little, and mostly through the demons we shared. But I know very well that his heart was good, and one thing is certain: Booth would not even have been started without those devils. Thanks, Daddy!

My good friend Jon Howe, who assured me that Booth would have starlets lining up to bear my children. We'll see how prescient he is, but he's one hell of a writer.

Finally, my dear friend Bliss Cochran, for copyediting this thing—no mean feat with my penchant for POV and tense shifts, not to mention inventing words. Thanks, Bliss!

## ABOUT THE AUTHOR

Timothy David Jones lives in Mexico, but he came of age in Louisiana. He fared but middling in high school, was thrown out of college for good reason, and was finally drafted into the Army, as were most other misfits of the day.

Following his time in service, Tim worked variously as a health and beauty aids route man, a carpenter, a machinist, a quality assurance tech, a welder, and a nuclear weapons research and development technician. When the Russians screwed up the R&D gig by dropping out of the Cold War, Tim retired, penniless, to the frozen wilds of northern Idaho. Here he lived peaceably if meagerly in a hand-built cabin for three years with outdoor plumbing and no running water.

After suffering from Seasonal Affective Disorder for several further years due to the persistent 500 foot winter overcast common to that region, he sold out and aimed his motorcycle south. He has lived in Mexico ever since, playing guitar and eating *tacos camarón.*

Tim has lamentably scant credentials as a writer. A few newspaper opinion pieces, yes. But, it should be noted, only one rejection slip—vindicating, perhaps, the principle of nothing ventured, nothing scorned. In any case, he has about as much business writing a novel as he has piloting jet aircraft or arguing before the Supreme Court.

Just the same, here it is…